DANNY AND RON ORLIS
IN THE
CANADIAN WILDERNESS

DANNY AND RON ORLIS

IN THE
CANADIAN WILDERNESS

BERNARD PALMER

Danny and Ron Orlis in the Canadian Wilderness
© 2024 by Bernard Palmer
All rights reserved. First edition 1960.
Second edition 2024.

Scripture quotations from The Authorized (King James) Version. Rights in the Authorized Version in the United Kingdom are vested in the Crown. Reproduced by permission of the Crown's patentee, Cambridge University Press.

Cover image: Adobe Firefly
Character illustrations: John Ball
Editor: Jon Fogdall

Aneko Press Youth

www.anekopress.com
Aneko Press, Life Sentence Publishing, and our logos are trademarks of Life Sentence Publishing, Inc.
203 E. Birch Street
P.O. Box 652
Abbotsford, WI 54405

JUVENILE FICTION / Religious / Christian / Action & Adventure
Paperback ISBN: 978-1-62245-990-2
eBook ISBN: 978-1-62245-991-9

10 9 8 7 6 5 4 3 2 1
Available where books are sold

CONTENTS

CHAPTER 1

SOMETHING NEW

Long narrow wisps of fog straggled across the Muskeg and Angle Bay, all that was left of the cold, gray shroud that had stolen in with the dawn. The wind still slept and the sun was somewhere behind Oak Island, stretching his golden arms upward to gild the eastern horizon. A blue heron glided majestically out of the sky and settled among the reeds, where he stood, one-legged, to fish for his morning meal. All the Angle was motionless and silent.

Danny Orlis opened the cabin door and stepped out into the chill air. He was tall and muscular, with a slight wave in his sandy-colored hair, and a grin that lurked about his lips. In the years since he had been away, he had grown taller and his face had taken on a finely chiseled look. The blue of his eyes had deepened.

On the bank of Pine Creek, he paused and looked about, as he had done so many times in years past.

He had left the cabin so quietly that the stately heron had not heard him, and was standing a scant 30 feet away. In the oak sapling to his left, a tree toad was laboriously moving over the rough bark hunting insects. A little higher in the tree a spider swung from one branch to another, busily spinning his web.

Danny took a deep breath and moved quietly out on the dock. Cap's and Jim's little packet boat was resting, motionless, at its mooring. While Danny watched, a school of minnows moved out from under it in search of food.

The sun was coming up and the last traces of the fog were melting away. Danny straightened and looked about. The grass was flourishing and tiny new leaves had suddenly burst forth on the trees to clothe the forest with green.

The most glorious season of the year!

Danny did not move until the cabin door slammed suddenly. The sound startled him. It startled the blue heron too. With one sweep of his powerful wings the great bird lifted himself noisily out of the water.

It was only Ron. He might have known.

"Jim awake?" the boy asked, approaching him.

Danny grinned. "If he isn't, he soon will be."

"What's the big idea of getting up in the middle of the night?" Ron asked, rubbing the sleep from his eyes.

"Mr. Pemberton will be here any day, and we'll have to start work on that film." Danny sat down on the dock, dangling his feet above the water. His brother joined him. "And there's a lot of work to do before he comes."

A lone mallard hen flew overhead, and from the little farmstead behind the Orlis cabin a dog barked.

Ron picked up a small pebble and tossed it into the water.

"What's this film job going to be like, Danny?"

"It's for the Tourist Bureau in Toronto. They want a film showing the wilderness and wildlife of Western Ontario to bring people into the area for vacations. It's a good deal if we can give them what they want."

Ron turned to face him. "But how did you get it?"

"Didn't you know that I'm a photographer?"

"Not that much of a photographer."

Danny laughed pleasantly. "I've been taking a correspondence course for a year and a half," he said. "It's about time to see whether I've learned anything."

"I guess I knew that too."

"A friend of mine tipped me off about the film the Tourist Bureau was going to make," Danny went on. "I wrote giving my qualifications and got the job."

"Sounds like fun. Maybe I can help."

"I've been counting on you. The Lord knew I would need all the money I can make this summer to get through Bible school next year. But I sure hate to be away from home again. Seems as though we never stay around here anymore."

"Maybe we could take some pictures right here,"

Ron suggested. "There are all kinds of animals and birds, and the country is wild enough for anybody."

"That's what I'm hoping. But we won't know for sure until Mr. Pemberton gets here. He's actually going to be in charge of the project."

Ron paused momentarily. "What's he like?" he asked at last.

Danny shook his head. "I haven't had any correspondence with him. The Tourist Bureau wrote and told me he'd be coming to take charge. That's all I know."

The boy grunted. "He'll probably be quite a dope. It'll most likely keep one of us busy looking after him so he doesn't get lost or hurt."

"You're an optimist."

"I've seen some of these officials before."

The sound of muffled voices came from inside the boat.

"Sounds like Jim and Cap are getting up," Danny said, standing. "Mother's probably got breakfast ready. We'd better go in, Ron."

"I'm hungry enough to eat a horse." They had left the dock and were walking up to the cabin when Ron stopped. "I just remembered what I came out to ask you about, Danny," he said. "Didn't you get a letter from Red Bostwick yesterday?"

"I got a letter from Newton Jonathan Edward Bostwick III," he corrected.

Ron grinned broadly, remembering the boy who had gone with them to Mexico the year before. "I forgot that he didn't like that name. What'd old Red want, anyway?"

Danny lowered his voice. "In his words, 'I want to have a conference with you and Ronald concerning a matter of the gravest importance.' "

Ron wrinkled his forehead. "That sounds like he's coming up here."

"He'll be here today," Danny said. "On the Fisheries' boat."

"You should have told me, Danny. I'd have dusted the dictionary."

The tourist season would be in full swing soon and the Orlis cabins were not ready. Danny, Ron and Roxie set to work, and were just finishing the second cabin when the Fisheries' boat followed the wooden buoys that marked the channel from Angle Bay up Pine Creek to the Orlis dock.

Newton Bostwick was standing on deck, grinning broadly and waving to Danny and Ron.

"There's Red!" Ron exclaimed, dropping his hammer.

Danny laid his tools on the table, and together the brothers started toward the dock.

"Hi, Red!" Ron shouted. "Hi!"

Newton scrambled off the boat as the lines were secured, and came running forward to meet them.

"Hi, Red! How are you?"

"The name," Newton said, shaking Ron's hand warmly, "is Newton Jonathan Edward Bostwick III."

"That's what I said," Ron told him, still smiling. "How're you doing, Red?"

Newton shrugged his shoulders. "I yield, Ronald. I shall never get you to desist from calling me 'Red.' From now on you have my complete and unqualified permission to call me Red – except on Sundays and legally recognized holidays."

"Now you're talkin'."

The other passenger went into the house with Mrs. Orlis, and the boys were alone on the dock.

Newton looked about carefully. "Is there a place where we might converse privately?"

Ron glanced into the Fisheries' boat and saw that the two-man crew was hard at work unloading lumber.

"You won't have to worry about talking here. Nobody's listening."

"Perhaps not," Newton replied doubtfully, "but we dare not risk it. As the immortal bard would say, 'even the walls have ears.'"

"Huh?" Ron demanded. "Oh–oh, I get it! You want that we should be alone."

"Precisely."

"And I have precisely the place," Danny broke in. "We'll go out in the trees behind the cabin."

"That'll never do," Ron said. "The chipmunks, you know. And that old tree toad."

Newton said nothing until they were in the trees back of the Orlis cabin. Although he was Ron's age and scarcely looked as old, he had graduated from high school the year before and had just finished his first year at a famed science institute. When they reached a safe distance from the cabin he stopped and turned solemnly to Danny and Ron.

"I have been informed that you received a commission to make a wildlife film for the Ontario Tourist Bureau," he almost whispered. "Was my information correct?"

"There's no secret about it," Danny told him. "We're going to start shooting as soon as Mr. Pemberton arrives."

"How did you find out about it?" Ron asked curiously.

"I only found it out about a week ago."

Newton eyed him archly.

"I have my contacts, Ronald," he informed him. And then he smiled briefly. "As a matter of fact, Uncle Harold Forester divulged the information. As soon as I heard it I exclaimed, figuratively of course, 'Eureka! The problem has been resolved! I shall see my very good friends, Daniel and Ronald Orlis!' "

Ron eyed him suspiciously. "I don't like the look in your eye, Red Bostwick. What's cooking?"

"Did either of you ever read the name of Dr. Ellsworth Desmond?" he asked. "Of course, you haven't," he added before they had time to speak. "You aren't familiar with scientific journals. Dr. Desmond is the father of a very close friend of mine."

"Yes?" There was a question in Danny's voice.

"For the past four years he has been wrestling with the problems involved in making a fast color film." Newton paused again and looked about. "At last he has succeeded. And–" he hesitated signifi-cantly, "we're going to give you the distinctive honor of being the first to try it."

"I don't think we'll have time, Newton," Danny told him. "We're going to start on this new publicity film as soon as Mr. Pemberton arrives, and he'll be here any day."

"But you do not understand, Daniel," Newton protested. "The fact that you are commissioned to do the film is precisely why I am here."

"We can't waste time on experimental film, Newton. It's going to be hard enough to get the sort of shots they want without being uncertain of our film."

"My dear Daniel! The film is experimental only inasmuch as it is not patented as yet and is not on the market. You have never seen such superb color, and fast! It is as fast as the wink of an electronic eye!"

Danny hesitated. "If the film has already been tested, why do you want us to test it again?"

"It has been tested and retested." Newton stepped closer. "This is for a very special test. Perhaps you are aware of the $50,000 cash award being offered by one of the major film companies for a color film with an ASA rating of 250."

Danny nodded.

"In order to win the award, we, Dr. Desmond, I mean, must submit a 30-minute film taken under every conceivable condition. We could make a print for you to turn over to Mr. Pemberton and use the original for the contest entry."

"But why doesn't Dr. Desmond take the pictures himself?" Danny asked. "After all, he's got a lot at stake."

"True." And then Newton's face grew more serious. "Dr. Desmond is partially paralyzed and in a wheelchair. He cannot shoot the film himself. That's why you must help us, Daniel!"

Danny was silent for a moment or two. "I'd like to help, Newton. Honestly I would. But I don't dare risk it unless that film's as good as you say it is."

Newton brightened quickly. "Would you try it, Daniel? Would you try one magazine of it?"

"How soon could you have it here? I've got to be ready to start shooting the day Pemberton arrives, you know."

"It so happens," Newton almost whispered, "that I have a magazine loaded with Code X in my pocket. Only we must be extremely careful. It has not been patented yet, and I have every reason to believe that someone is trying to steal it!"

CHAPTER 2

INTRUDERS

Ron's interest quickened. "What makes you think someone is after the film, Red?" he asked.

"I *know* they are attempting to steal it," Newton continued seriously. "They broke into Dr. Desmond's laboratory in the Cities. His wife returned home unexpectedly and surprised them there. They *almost* got the formula."

"But if it's so valuable, why doesn't this Dr. Desmond get a patent on it?" Danny asked. "That's what a patent is for, to give protection to the inventor."

"A patent requires money. The services of a patent attorney must be secured. The files must be searched to be sure the film is original. And Dr. Desmond has exhausted all his credit, and more too, in perfecting the film. He could not raise a hundred dollars, Daniel."

"That does put a different light on it."

"And one more thing. Dr. Desmond is a strong Christian. That is the principal reason he launched the film project. So missionaries would have a film with wide latitude and speed enough for even the poorest conditions."

Danny straightened. "You win, Newton. We'll go out tomorrow and see what this film of yours will do."

The three boys got their gear together that afternoon and the following morning at dawn shoved off in one of the canoes. It was a long trip over to the Canadian Customs, and it was almost noon when they made the portage out of the Lake of the Woods into Shoal Lake.

"How come we're going way over here?" Newton asked, panting. "Can't we take pictures a little closer to home?"

"Sure thing," Danny told him, "but I know Pemberton is going to want some moose shots. And it might be a little difficult for us to locate a good, big bull moose on short order. I thought we'd come over here and take a look around."

They finished hauling the canoe and their gear across the portage and headed out into the shallow, island-studded lake. Now and then Newton glanced over his shoulder expectantly.

"What do you expect to see out here?" Ron asked him. "Gangsters with tommy guns?"

"I remember quite well what happened to us the last time we found ourselves together."

"But that was in Mexico," Ron replied, laughing. "You won't find anything like that around here."

"I hope you are right, Ronald. I sincerely hope that you are right."

Newton took his turn at the paddle. As they stopped to rest after half an hour on the lake he turned to Danny.

"Are there many fishermen in this general area at this time of year?" he asked. There was a strange little catch in his voice.

Danny shook his head. "The fishermen and tourists won't be along for another month, in any force, that is."

Newton's eyes widened.

"Then who are those fellows behind us?"

Danny turned to see two men at the portage. They were putting their canoe into the water and were loading it with camping equipment.

"We're too far away to see if it's anybody I know. But it could be the game warden, or someone from the forestry service, or even a couple of Mounties. I don't think it's anything to worry about."

But Newton was unconvinced.

"Those two don't act as if they know how to handle a canoe."

"That's right, Danny," Ron put in. "They're as clumsy as a Chicago tourist."

"But that still doesn't mean they couldn't be fisher-men," Danny insisted. "A few fellows brave the cold to get in on the spring fishing."

"There's one way we can find out whether or not they're following us," Ron put in. "All we've got to do is start ducking around among these islands. If they zigzag with us, they're after us."

"Ronald!" Newton exclaimed quickly. "In your quaint way, you are a genius. A veritable genius!"

Ron smiled broadly. "Indubitably, my friend. Indubitably."

They began to paddle faster, heading around first one island and then another, soon losing sight of the other canoe. Newton kept looking back. It was not until they had gone a mile or more and circled several islands that he sighed deeply.

"There. We have eluded them."

"To be honest with you, Newton," Danny said, "I don't think they were following us in the first place. How would they know about you and the film? There just isn't any connection."

Newton hesitated for a long minute.

"I am afraid I permitted you to labor under a slight delusion, Daniel," he began uncertainly.

"What do you mean?"

"I am not entirely positive," he went on, "but I am somewhat afraid that I was followed to Angle Inlet. I observed two men as I left Dr. Desmond's apartment house. The same two characters, I was about to do them the injustice of calling them gentlemen, got on the bus at Minneapolis and rode to Warroad."

"Are you sure?" Danny demanded.

"They were either the same men or looked disturbingly like them."

"Boy, you sure handed us something, Red!" Ron said, but his eyes were glowing.

"That does put a different slant on things," Danny said.

They camped that night on a small out-of-the-way island in Shoal Lake. Danny and Ron pitched the tent and ditched it carefully, while Newton carried up the gear from the lake and suspended the knapsacks full of food from tree limbs so they were eight or nine feet off the ground.

"There," he said when he had finished, "does that suit you?"

"Capital, Red, old boy," Ron replied. "Now we won't have to worry about a bear getting our grub."

"That is the most minute among my worries at the moment," Newton answered. "You aren't going to build a fire tonight, are you? With those fellows in the area?"

"Of course, we're going to have a fire," Ron said. "If you think *I'm* going to eat cold beans tonight just because you think somebody's following you, you've got another guess due you, Red, old bean."

"We'll have a fire," Danny said, grinning, "but you won't have to worry about anyone seeing it. I've got a rack and some canned heat."

"And if you're still afraid someone might see it, Red, we could take it in the tent or hold blankets around it."

"Jest, if you wish, Ronald Orlis," Newton countered. "But be sure and keep up your guard."

The boys had their devotions that evening and turned in before dark. Ron was a little nervous, although he wouldn't have admitted it to Newton, but he closed his eyes. And the next thing he knew it was morning.

"Well, Red," he said brightly as they cooked breakfast, "we got through last night without having your big, bold, bad men gobble us up."

"And fortunate we were," Newton replied. "Most fortunate."

That morning they nosed around among the islands in the canoe, looking for something to photograph. With the binoculars, Ron spotted two or three deer, but Danny vetoed going after them with the camera.

"By the time we get over there they'll be back in the brush," he said, "or in the shadows so far that we wouldn't be able to get a good picture."

"Just try it," Newton urged. "Go over and try a scene or two. That's just the sort of stuff this film is for."

"I'd rather try it under normal conditions first," Danny told him. "I brought a magazine of regular color film along too. We'll shoot a few feet with each and compare them. That way we'll know whether your film's any good."

About noon Danny took a few feet of scenery with each film, but they had seen no animals worth photographing.

"I don't think we're going to take any pictures," Ron said disappointedly. "And we're sure not going to find any moose around here. I haven't seen any moose sign, have you, Danny?"

His brother shook his head.

The rest of the afternoon passed quickly. And the sun was almost hidden behind the trees on the horizon when they came upon a beaver busily at work.

"Look!" Ron exclaimed excitedly. "And right out in the open!"

Both Newton and Danny turned to stare at the little animal.

"Have you a telescopic lens?" Newton asked.

Danny nodded. "But we could never get a decent picture in light like this."

"Give it a chance, Daniel! We'll get you in as close as you want to be. Just get that beaver in the viewfinder and start clicking off the film."

The beaver didn't even know they were around as Ron and Newton pushed the canoe forward silently. He felled a small tree and floated it into his dam. By this time, the boys had moved so close they could see his broad flat tail and his big teeth that served as an ax.

Finally, Danny, who had been crouching in the prow of the canoe, turned to his companions. "That ought to be enough of that. Back away as silently as you can. I don't want to disturb him."

"That ought to make a wonderful scene," Newton exclaimed.

"If the film's any good," Ron put in.

"You needn't fret yourself about that," Newton answered confidently. "The film is good."

The following morning, Danny loaded the camera

with a fresh magazine of regular color film and insisted on going back to the beaver dam.

"But we've already got all the pictures you'll want of that," Newton protested.

"It isn't often a fellow gets a chance to get pictures of a beaver at work. I want to try some shots with this film in bright sunlight to be sure of some good pictures."

Newton frowned. "You pain me, Daniel. What is the difficulty? Do you still persist in thinking that I am exaggerating the truth when I tell you about Dr. Desmond's film?"

"I believe you, Newton," Danny said.

"But he still wants to be sure of some good pictures," Ron broke in laughing.

They moved stealthily up the creek where the beaver had been working. He was there, as before, in a little patch of bright sunlight.

"Easy now, fellows," Danny whispered tensely.

But the beaver was more cautious and timid than before. He worked a little, then raised on his haunches and looked about.

"Closer," Danny whispered.

Ron and Newton inched the canoe forward.

Danny had only shot eight or ten feet of film when the beaver heard the clicking of the camera. His head went up, and he froze for an instant, listening. Then he streaked for the water and in one blur of motion dived out of sight.

"Gone!" Ron exclaimed disappointedly.

"Those pictures we took last night will be better anyway," Newton exclaimed.

When they got back to the camp, Ron stopped and stared.

"Danny!" he cried.

His brother and Newton came running up beside him. The knapsack that had contained the film was open on the ground!

"Those men!" Newton moaned. "They've been here!" *"And the film is gone!"*

CHAPTER 3

IT WORKED!

Silence hung over the little camp. Danny picked up the knapsack and looked at it.

"You were right, Newton," he said at last. "I've got to confess that I thought you were exaggerating when you kept worrying about those fellows all the time."

"Of course, I was correct," the red-haired boy retorted. "I had observed them closely. I was positive that they had been following me, and that they would be following us."

"But what are we going to do about it?" Ron broke in. "We can't let them get away with that film!"

Danny pursed his lips. "We're going to have a rough time following them," he said. "They came by canoe and left the same way. There's no way of tracking them."

"But we've got to do something, Danny!" Ron protested. "We can't let them get away with it!"

And then Newton began to smile. "We would be in an extremely difficult position," he said, "even though only a portion of the secret is contained in the film itself, and the balance lies in the developing."

"What do you mean?" Ron demanded suspiciously. "What are you talking about?"

"As I informed you a moment ago," Newton continued with tantalizing slowness, "we would be in an extremely difficult position, except for the fact that I possessed sufficient foresight to have anticipated just such a move as this on the part of our adversaries." He fished a film magazine from his pocket and held it up.

"You've got the film?" Danny shouted.

"Precisely," Newton answered. "I took the liberty of placing this magazine containing Dr. Desmond's film, Code X, in my pocket, and the magazine with the partially exposed roll of regular color film in the knapsack."

The Orlis boys grinned in spite of themselves.

"Red Bostwick!" Ron exclaimed. "If you pull a trick like that on us again, I'll clobber you."

Newton put the film back in his pocket. "That, Ronald," he said significantly, "would be most unwise. I am too fat to run and too slow to fight."

"Right now, we've got to decide what we're going to do," Danny broke in. "Those fellows will find out that they stole the wrong film. And when they do, I'm afraid they'll be back."

Newton's eyes widened.

"Do you really think so?"

"We could get in touch with the Mounties in Kenora," Ron suggested. "Those guys stole our film. They could get into trouble for that."

Danny pulled at the lobe of his ear, thoughtfully. "What could we tell them?" he asked. "We've been robbed, all right, but the film isn't worth more than a few dollars. That's not enough for the authorities to come rushing out here to investigate. And we don't have any evidence at all that those two men did it."

The boys had planned on staying at Shoal Lake another day or two, but now Danny decided to go back to Angle Inlet.

"It would probably be best anyway. Tex will be in with the mail tomorrow. We can send this roll of film down to Dr. Desmond for development while we wait for Mr. Pemberton."

Newton wiped the smile from his face and drew himself up to his full five feet three inches.

"I find it distasteful to boast, Daniel," he said, "but it will be unnecessary for us to send the film anywhere for development. I have all the necessary equipment with me."

"You mean Dr. Desmond trusted you with the secret of developing his film?" Ron asked incredulously.

"My dear Ronald, I not only am entrusted with it, I helped develop it."

Ron shook his head in wonderment.

Back at the Angle, Newton made one of the little tourist cabins into a dark room with Ron's help.

"You didn't say anything to your folks about those men, did you, Ronald?" Newton asked as they worked.

The boy shook his head.

"It is just as well that only we three know about it."

"They would keep their eyes open for strangers too," Ron said, "if we told them about it and described the two men who followed you."

"I knew I was being followed, Ronald," Newton told him, "but those fellows were clever enough to remain in the shadows, so I didn't get a good look at them. I haven't the slightest idea what they look like."

When Newton was finally satisfied that the room had been made as dark as possible he shoved Ron toward the door.

"I no longer require your services, Ronald, old chap. When I have finished I will inform you."

"But you can trust me," the boy protested.

"I quite realize that. Especially when you have no information to divulge."

Ron snorted and, muttering under his breath, stalked out of the cabin, and Newton locked the door.

It was almost an hour before he came to the door and called to Ron.

"Get Danny," the young scientist said. "I have something to show you."

The two boys hurried into the cabin and Danny took the strip of the film.

"It is still quite wet," Newton said, "but if you hold

it up to the light you will see that I did not exaggerate the good qualities of Dr. Desmond's new product."

Danny moved to the doorway and held the film between him and the sky.

"Say!" he exclaimed. "This is not bad!"

"Not bad?" Newton echoed. "It is perfect! Absolutely perfect! Notice the sharp detail, the normal flesh tones, and the natural color of the grass and trees. And you must keep in mind that the pictures were exposed under most adverse conditions."

The film looked even better when it was projected on the screen.

When they had finished screening it, Danny looked at his watch. "We've got some work to do, Ronald," he said. "I had a wire from Mr. Pemberton. He's due here in the morning and wants to get right to work. We've got to get busy or we won't be ready for him."

"I do not like to disturb your thinking, Daniel," Newton said, his eyes sparkling, "but you haven't yet given me a decision concerning our film."

"I'd like to use it, Newton," Danny told him. "It has wonderful possibilities. And in shooting ani-mal pictures we need the latitude this film seems to have. But Mr. Pemberton is going to be here tomor-row, and we'll have to get right to work. I'm afraid there isn't time to get a supply of your film. And, of course, once we start shooting with one film we will be forced to continue. The changes in color would be too noticeable."

"I quite agree. The color in our film is so much more natural that regular film would be much too garish and unreal." He smiled briefly. "However, I am also prepared for that emergency. I brought along a small supply of film, and more will be coming before that is exposed."

"You think of everything, don't you?"

"I try, Daniel. I try."

"There's one more thing," Danny said. "If we use this film, we've got to know that we'll be able to get enough of it to finish the job. Can Dr. Desmond supply it to us?"

"He not only can supply it, but he will. He assured me that he could make shipments from time to time to keep you in film."

Danny smiled. "Fine."

"We must not permit Pemberton to learn anything about the film," Newton said. "I gave my word that only you and Ron would be informed. Dr. Desmond is a fine fellow, and a solid Christian, but most suspicious."

"Sounds to me as though he has a right to be," Ron said, "the way those guys are trying to steal his invention."

"True. True."

"You can count on us," Ron answered brightly. "Mum's the word."

Newton scowled at him with mock sternness. "That is what I have been trying to tell you, Ronald. There had better not be any word."

CHAPTER 4

A COLD DUCKING

The Orlis family and Newton had just finished breakfast at Angle Inlet the following morning when a light float plane skimmed over the trees and banked for a landing on the wide creek.

"Well," Danny said, pushing back from the table and getting to his feet, "it looks as though the Pembertons are right on time."

"Did you say the Pembertons?" Ron asked. "Plural? I thought there was just one Pemberton coming. Or is he twins?"

"Very funny, my little brother," Danny said, grinning. "Very funny."

"I would like to inform you, Ronald," Newton said, "that I pursued this same line of questioning last evening. I don't think that I am revealing any secrets to announce that this Mr. Pemberton is also bringing along his 16-year-old son."

"To tell you the truth," Danny answered, eyes twinkling, "I decided not to say anything about it in front of Roxie. Didn't want her getting any ideas."

Roxie's cheeks colored daintily as everybody else began to laugh.

"Danny!" she exclaimed.

"I know how to handle that bird," Ron broke in. "It's easy. As soon as he gets here I'll march right up to him and say, 'Now listen here, I want you to leave my twin sister alone. She's allergic to fellows!' "

By this time Roxie was blushing scarlet. "Ron Orlis!" she exclaimed. "Don't you dare! You stay out of this!"

They all began to laugh uproariously.

"I mean–I mean–"

"We know exactly what you mean."

"We know what you mean, Roxie," Danny told her.

"Danny Orlis!" she retorted hotly. "You're getting just as bad as Ron when it comes to teasing!"

"What do you mean by that?" Ron asked. "I learned it from him."

Newton had slipped away from the table and was standing at the kitchen window watching the little plane.

"They're coming in for a landing," he said. "Now remember what I warned you about, Ron and Danny."

Mr. and Mrs. Orlis looked at Newton but said nothing.

The family started for the door to meet their guests. All, that is, except Roxie.

"Come on, Roxie," Ron called to her. "You've got to come along and see what your new conquest looks like."

"I–I'm not going to move a step."

"He's going to be terribly disappointed. Danny's probably written him all about you."

"I–I'm not going out there and let you embarrass me."

"Come on, Roxie!" Danny told her. "I'm not going to say anything, and neither is Ron. If he does, he'll have to answer to me."

She joined the others, reluctantly.

By the time they reached the bank of the stream, the little plane had touched down and was taxiing toward the dock.

"Better bring her in over here," Carl Orlis called to the pilot. "We've got some ties anchored here."

Pemberton brought the plane expertly to the beach, almost exactly in front of Mr. Orlis. Danny and Ron grabbed the struts and pulled it in until the floats were touching the bank.

While the graying, thin-faced producer was reaching for a briefcase behind him, the door on the other side of the plane opened and a lanky, thin-faced lad about the twins' age got out. He stood on the float momentarily, running his thin fingers across his sallow face, and surveying the cabins and the forest behind them.

"Some dump!" he exclaimed. "I should have known better than to come out here. I should have stayed in Toronto."

Mr. Pemberton was busy talking with Carl Orlis and Danny. Ron went over to the newcomer.

"Hi."

The other boy did not answer him. "Some dump," he repeated. "That's all I can say."

"Oh, it's not so bad up here!" Ron told him. "At least we like it."

The newcomer snorted contemptuously. "Some people can be satisfied with anything."

Words flew to Ron's lips, and it was all he could do to force them down. "You'd better come into the house," he said. "Mother has breakfast ready."

Eldon Pemberton wrinkled his nose distastefully. He stepped off the float and stood beside Ron, looking at the barn, the machine shed, and the small log building that served as a post office.

"In which of these buildings do you eat?" Eldon wanted to know. "And which do you keep for your cow?"

Ron swallowed hard and dug his clenched fists deep into his pocket. There were times when it was hard to act like a Christian.

"Come on," he said, trying to sound pleasant, "and I'll show you."

Newton fell in beside them.

"Do you go along with your dad on trips very often?" Ron asked.

"Go with him often?" the newcomer echoed. "I'll have you know that I'm his personal assistant when I'm not in school. Usually, we are working with professional photographers in a–a civilized place. I don't know why he took this assignment. I know we wouldn't be wasting our time in a hole like this if I had my way."

"I am quite positive you are making a snap judgment without due consideration," Newton said, "that you are leaping to a conclusion you will not desire to maintain after you have sojourned here for a brief period."

Eldon's mouth dropped open and he whirled to face Newton.

"Huh?" he blurted.

"What Red means is that you'll change your mind after you have been here a couple of days."

"Precisely," Newton added. "Precisely."

Eldon was still staring at him. "Do–do you always talk that way, Red?"

"I will thank you not to call me 'Red,' " Newton said without rancor. Only Ron saw that his eyes were twinkling merrily. "I have made a special dispensation in the case of Ronald. He has my permission to address me by the odious nickname of 'Red.' "

"Because I kept calling him 'Red' anyway," the boy explained.

"To you, as to all others," Newton continued, "my name is Newton Bostwick. Newton Jonathan Edward Bostwick III."

Danny and Mr. Pemberton were right behind them as they went into the kitchen.

"I'm glad to know that you're ready to go to work, Danny," the producer said. "We've got a lot to do."

"We could begin today," Danny told him, "unless you'd like to rest for a while."

"I don't think we'll want to begin photographing today," Gil Pemberton answered, "but as we flew over, I saw a lot of interesting country to photograph. I'd like to take a look at some of it from the ground."

"Good. We'll get out the 'Scappoose' and start as soon as you've had a cup of coffee."

"Want to go along, Eldon?"

"Oh, I don't think so, Dad!" the boy said. "When you've seen one tree you've seen them all."

The smile left Mr. Pemberton's face, but he said nothing.

Danny took Gil Pemberton out in the 'Scappoose', and they cruised around Big and Little McCoy Islands, took a run over to Magnuson's Island and American Point, and to the Canadian Customs just off Oak.

"It's beautiful, Orlis. I can scarcely wait to get started."

Danny smiled. There was something about the tall, angular man that he liked instinctively.

"Do you suppose your brother is angry with Eldon?" Gil asked after a time.

"Ron isn't easily hurt."

"I want to apologize to him," Mr. Pemberton continued.

"You won't have to do that."

"I know, but I want to. I'm afraid Eldon is something of a problem. You see, his mother left us when he was a baby and I've had to rear him myself. I'm afraid I haven't been as stern as I should have been. Now we're seeing the result of it."

Danny nodded understandingly.

"I got a little rundown on you and your brother from the fellows at the Tourist Bureau. They told me you were young and clean-cut. I thought that associating with the two of you, and being out here in the wilderness this way, might have its effect on him."

"We'll certainly do what we can to help," Danny answered. "I'll talk to Ron when we get back."

"That will be fine."

"Of course, there isn't a lot that we can do by ourselves."

Pemberton's eyebrows arched quizzically.

"We'll do the best we can," Danny went on. "But being a good example to Eldon, and his being here in the wilderness isn't going to do much of itself."

"I'm afraid I don't follow you."

"What I'm trying to say is this, Gil. The only thing that can change Eldon is the thing that has changed Ron and me, and anyone else who has come face to face with the problem of sin and has conquered it."

Anger flickered momentarily in Gil Pemberton's eyes. "That sounds very suspiciously like religion." Disapproval was in his voice.

"Not religion," Danny corrected. "Christianity! We have allowed the Lord Jesus to conquer the sin in our lives. We have recognized that we were sinners and needed a Savior, and have put our trust in Him. That's what Eldon needs. When he does that, you'll see a change in him."

Gil Pemberton was looking beyond Danny, and for a long while he did not answer.

"I'd like to see Eldon different," he said at last. "Even now I don't know what to do or how to handle him. But to be honest with you, I don't think much of this religion business."

He paused. Danny waited patiently.

"I don't want him to lean on a crutch. I want him to stand on his own two feet, and to face the world the way I've had to." There was unaccountable bitterness in his voice. "He doesn't need these things you've been talking about. All he's got to do is get hold of himself."

Danny would have continued the conversation, but he saw the anger in Gil Pemberton's eyes and decided against it.

"I'll be glad to do what I can to help Eldon," he said softly, "and I know that Ron and Newton will help too."

The anger faded and died away. "I'm sorry for that outburst, lad. I know you meant well enough. But it just happens to be the way I feel about religion."

And then, abruptly, he changed the subject.

The following morning, Ron and Newton packed their fishing gear and cooking kit in the boat while Mrs. Orlis and Roxie prepared breakfast. When devotions were over the five of them set out in a boat, pulling a canoe behind.

"If we're not going to be back before night, who's going to cook on this expedition?" Eldon asked.

"We usually take turns," Danny explained.

"That doesn't sound like such a hot idea to me."

They cleared Customs and went over to Monument Bay, where they set up a little base of operations.

"As long as we're working this close to home we'd just as well go back to Angle Inlet to sleep," Danny said, "but we can leave our canoe and gear here. It'll save us a lot of work loading and unloading it every day."

"Sounds like a good idea to me."

"What I want to know," Eldon put in, "is when are you going to show us a moose? I happen to know that they're going to insist on some moose pictures."

"We'll probably have to go farther north for them," Danny told him. "It's been several weeks since anyone has seen a moose around here."

"We were even up to Shoal Lake a few days ago," Ron said, "scouting around for moose signs, but we didn't see any. That liver fluke must have thinned them down a lot."

"That's a likely story. I don't think there ever were any moose around here. You probably just lied about it in order to get the job."

"We'll show you a moose, all right," Ron said.

Mr. Pemberton decided that he wanted to get some scenic pictures first, and Danny took the party to the north end of Monument Bay among the picturesque islands.

When dinner time came, they went ashore. Danny broke five matches into varying lengths and held them out. Eldon got the short one.

"It looks as though I'm the goat on this expedition," he growled. "What did you do, Orlis? Frame me?"

"It isn't any more difficult to prepare the first meal than it is the last," Newton broke in. "In fact, there is something rewarding in the thought that the disagreeable task has been completed."

"If that's the way you feel about it you can have my turn."

"I should like very much to take it, but I would not want to cheat you of the joy that will be yours."

"Joy!" Eldon snorted. "I've got another name for it."

They set up the camp stove on a flat rock next to the water. Ron showed Eldon how to light it, and Danny helped get out the cooking kit.

"If I'd known I was going to get in on any mess like this I'd have stayed home," Eldon grumbled.

With that he took a step or two backward. Danny shouted in warning! But he was too late! Eldon stumbled off the rock into the icy water!

CHAPTER 5

UPWIND!

Help!" Eldon Pemberton yelped plaintively as he splashed about in the icy water. "Help! Help!" Quickly Danny Orlis snatched an oar from the boat and held it out to Eldon. But it was apparent that he didn't need it. He swam to shore, and Danny and Gil Pemberton pulled him out.

"Do you always go swimming with your clothes on?" Ron asked, laughing.

Eldon glared at him. The goose pimples had raised on his arms, and he was shivering in the brisk wind. Danny got a jacket and tossed it to him.

"I wasn't aware that you intended to bathe in the lake before cooking," Newton said seriously. "You won't need to do that before every meal. If you wash your hands thoroughly that will suffice."

Danny and Gil snorted.

"Very funny," Eldon said bitterly. "I'm about to die laughing."

Ron picked up the camera.

"Eldon." He lined up young Pemberton in the viewfinder. "We didn't have the camera out when you did that. Would you please go through it again?"

Newton snickered explosively.

"I said nobody was going to make fun of me," Eldon gritted. "And I meant it." He moved toward Ron, his fists clenched menacingly.

"Now none of that!" Gil Pemberton ordered. He and Danny both grabbed Eldon at the same time, pinning his arms to his sides.

"Let me go!" He wriggled to free himself.

"Ron wasn't laughing at you, Eldon," Danny told him, struggling to keep his voice free from anger. "And neither were any of the rest of us. It just happened to be funny the way you fell in the water and came up, spouting like a whale. So we laughed. There wasn't anything personal."

"It didn't seem very funny to me."

"That's enough, Eldon," his dad said sternly. "Now get back to your cooking."

"But I'm all wet, and about to freeze."

"You'll dry out."

Eldon glared at Ron momentarily, then turned back to the fire.

When they sat down to eat, Danny asked the blessing. Gil Pemberton bowed his head, but Eldon stared at Danny.

"Ron," Danny said that evening when they were back at Angle Inlet, "I'm sorry about what happened today. And so is Mr. Pemberton. He asked me to apologize for him."

"I didn't mean any harm, Danny," Ron told him. "I plan on telling Eldon I'm sorry I laughed at him, but I thought I'd better wait until he cooled down a little."

"And, Ron," Danny added, "we ought to pray for him. I'm afraid that he's a very mixed-up and unhappy fellow."

Ron got his chance to apologize to Eldon the following day. But the tall easterner only stared at him.

"That doesn't mean a thing to me, Orlis. I didn't ask for your apology, and I don't want it. I can get along without the whole lot of you."

"I know that," Ron told him. "But I want you to know that I didn't intend to make fun of you. And I'm sorry that you took offense at it."

His companion's eyes narrowed.

"Are you finished?"

"I–I guess so."

Without saying another word, Eldon turned on his heel and stalked away.

Mr. Orlis had some work he wanted Ron and Newton to do that morning, so Danny took the two Pembertons in the canoe and went over to the Canadian side of the Bay.

"I think we can find some deer over here," Danny explained. "Dad was telling me about seeing a doe and her twins over this way a week or so ago. They travel around quite a little, but we ought to be able to find them if we look a bit."

Eldon surveyed the brush-choked mainland skeptically. "You don't mean you're getting out to walk in that, do you?" he asked. "In all those mosquitoes?"

Danny laughed. "After a week or two you'll get so you won't even notice them. At least that's what people try to tell you."

It was a long, grueling hike through the brush. Danny led the way and Gil Pemberton and Eldon followed. Sweat streaked their faces and their legs began to ache.

"I tell you I'm not going to walk another step in this stuff," Eldon said panting wearily. "I'm going back to the canoe."

"You can't go back alone," Danny told him firmly.

Eldon's eyes blazed his defiance. "I can if I want to. Nobody tells *me* what to do."

"Somebody's going to tell you what to do out here, Eldon. Unless you've had a lot more experience in the woods than I think you've had, you wouldn't be able to go a quarter mile without getting lost."

"That's what you think." Nevertheless, Eldon followed along behind them, grumbling to himself as he stumbled over deadfalls and rocks. "When are we going back?" he asked plaintively. "I can't walk another step."

For answer Danny turned quickly and placed a warning finger on his lips.

Gil Pemberton crouched instinctively.

"There they are," Danny whispered. "Just ahead of us."

He surveyed the situation quickly. The old doe and her fawns were upwind. That meant she wouldn't be able to get their scent.

Danny crept forward stealthily.

"What kind of a photographer is he, Dad?" Eldon said in a stage whisper. "You can't take color pictures in shadows like this."

What Eldon said was true. Almost prayerfully Danny began to take pictures. What if that first reel of film had been a fluke? What if it wouldn't work with unfavorable light conditions again? Would Pemberton wire Toronto that he didn't know enough about photography to handle the job?

Grimly, Danny forced such thoughts from his mind as he began to shoot. It was almost fifteen minutes later that he turned back to his companions.

"I think we've got all we need of those deer," he said. "We can always find deer if you need more pictures."

Gil Pemberton said nothing until they were back in the canoe. "You certainly don't think you got any pictures in that deep shade, do you?" he asked.

Danny could guess what he was thinking.

"We'll soon know. Newton will develop the film as soon as we get back."

"That boy?" Gil echoed. "You mean you'll trust him to develop your film? That's preposterous!"

"I told you, Dad! I told you they've been faking. They don't know a thing about photography."

Danny smiled. "We'll see in an hour or so."

Newton took the film out to the cabin that served as a dark room and set to work.

Danny and the others waited anxiously.

When he finally finished, he stuck his head out the cabin door and yelled.

Gil Pemberton almost snatched the film from Newton's chubby fingers and held it up to the light.

"This–this isn't the film we took this afternoon," he said, his voice thick with doubt.

"Unfortunately, I cannot answer that question," Newton said, "since I was not present when the film was exposed. But I can assure you it is the film that Daniel handed me when you returned from your expedition into the muskeg."

"Why, I–I've never seen anything like it!" Gil Pemberton exclaimed. "It's perfectly exposed, and the colors are truer and more natural than any film I've ever seen." He turned to Danny. "This isn't regular commercial film, is it?"

Danny glanced at Newton, who was shaking his head with vigor.

"I'm sorry, Mr. Pemberton," Danny answered reluctantly. "But I'm not at liberty to tell you anything about the film right now."

"We're in on this the same as you are," Eldon insisted.

Danny shook his head.

"I may be able to tell you more later. But at the moment I'm not at liberty to say anything."

The boy scowled angrily.

CHAPTER 6

MEN IN DISTRESS

Cap and Jim were at Angle Inlet that evening with three passengers who were staying overnight. Everyone was crowded into the small living room.

"I still think you ought to tell us about that film, Danny," Eldon said loudly.

Danny turned as though he hadn't heard Eldon, and answered the question of the man beside him.

"What is it with this film, Danny?" the boy persisted. "How can you take good pictures under such lousy conditions? Is it something new?"

"I've told all I'm at liberty to tell you, Eldon," Danny answered.

"You can tell us if you want to. You're just being stubborn." Eldon's lower lip curled petulantly.

Newton Bostwick stiffened. He glanced quickly from one guest to another, fearfully. But they were querying Mr. Orlis about the fishing and hadn't even heard. Or had they?

"It's a fine thing!" Eldon continued. "Here Dad and I are producing this publicity film for the Ontario Tourist Bureau–" He paused for his words to register with the others, and looked about, smiling condescendingly. "We're producing this publicity film for the Ontario Tourist Bureau and you won't even tell us what sort of film you're using."

By this time everyone had turned toward him.

"What is it, Danny?"

Danny squirmed miserably.

Mrs. Orlis came in just then and announced that dinner was ready. Newton looked at Ron and sighed his relief.

"I intend to take a position next to that curious individual," he whispered. "And if he starts his interrogation again, I'm going to kick him in the shins so hard that he'll forget what he's saying."

"Danny," Eldon began again, "about that–"

"Oh, Cap!" Ron broke in hurriedly. "I was wondering, did you have a rough crossing today?"

Cap looked at him incredulously. "What's the matter with you, boy? The lake was like a mirror."

Ron's cheeks colored slightly and he looked down at his plate.

"I was going to ask you, Danny," Eldon began again, "what about that–"

"You should have observed the loons we discovered today, Mr. Pemberton," Newton said loudly.

"Now there's something you ought to include in your pictures. They intrigue me."

The conversation drifted to loons and birds. Eldon glared at Newton helplessly.

Half a dozen times during the course of the evening he tried to needle Danny about the film. But each time Ron or Newton broke in on him, asking someone a question or deftly changing the subject.

At last the meal was over and Carl Orlis turned to Ron. "Would you please get my Bible and glasses off the buffet?"

"Do you mean you're going to read the Bible *again?*" Eldon demanded sarcastically.

"It's a custom with us," Mr. Orlis explained gently.

"And I think it is a wonderful custom," one of the guests said. "My wife and I make it a habit to read the Word of God every night before going to bed. It has made our marriage what it is today."

"We read the Bible," Mr. Orlis went on, "because we have taken the Lord Jesus as our Savior and with His help we strive to live as He wants us to. We read His Word for understanding and guidance and strength."

Eldon would have countered caustically, but his father glanced at him and shook his head.

After Mr. Orlis had read the Bible and had finished praying, Eldon pushed haughtily back from the table.

"If the sermon's over, I think I'll turn in."

The others sat around for a while talking. Then, one by one, they drifted off to bed.

Danny, Ron, and Newton got together for a couple of minutes in the cabin where the younger boys were sleeping.

"I wish to inform you, fellows," Newton began, lowering his voice, "that I am tremendously concerned about the way Eldon persisted in questioning us about the film. He perceives that we have something quite different."

"You're right about that, Red," Ron answered. "I thought we were going to run out of things to break in on him. Old Cap about swallowed his teeth when I asked if he'd had a rough crossing."

"That was not the most intelligent question you could have asked."

"I know it, Red, but I'm not a brain like you are. And it was the only thing I could think of."

"I've been doing some thinking about this thing, Newton," Danny ventured. "It's up to you, of course, but don't you think it would be better if we could tell Eldon a little something about the film? That would satisfy him and maybe he'd keep his mouth shut."

Newton shook his head. "Dr. Desmond extracted a vow from me that I would not divulge the existence of the film to anyone, except you two."

"I guess that takes care of that then." Danny walked over to the doorway and looked out into the still night air. "But Eldon is curious and so is Gil. They're both going to ask a lot of questions."

There was a short silence.

"Do you think those fellows will make another try for it, Danny," Ron asked, "when they find out we tricked them?"

"That Newton Jonathan Edward Bostwick III tricked them, you mean," Newton corrected.

"I'm afraid they will, Ron," Danny answered. "If that film continues to prove out, it ought to be worth a small fortune."

Newton and Ron were standing beside him.

"Maybe we ought to get up to our base camp north of Kenora just as soon as we can," Ron suggested. "Before those guys discover that they stole the wrong film."

"That, Ronald Orlis, expresses my thinking exactly."

"Unfortunately, it doesn't express Gil Pemberton's thinking," Danny told them. "He still got quite a lot of subjects to photograph around here. He isn't ready to go up north yet, or so he says. And there's nothing I can do about it."

A strange look crossed Newton's face. "Could it be that Mr. Pemberton is in collaboration with those scoundrels who are trying to rob Dr. Desmond?"

"You've been reading too much Sherlock Holmes, Newton," Danny replied.

"I don't know," Ron put in. "I'm getting so I don't trust anyone anymore. Do you think we can hurry him up?"

"We'll do what we can."

The following morning before breakfast, Eldon went out to the little barn where Ron was milking the cow. He stood there for several minutes, leaning against the door.

"Say, Ron," he began, his voice condescending, "what do you know about that film Danny's using?"

Ron felt the blood rush to his cheeks.

"Not much."

"There's something fishy about it. They can't fool me." "I don't know much about cameras or film either." "I've been out with Dad enough to know that if Danny had been using ordinary film, he wouldn't have gotten a thing yesterday. Come on, tell me about it."

"I'm sorry, Eldon," Ron said, "but I can't tell you a thing about it. You'll have to ask Danny."

"He won't tell me anything either." He kicked the door sill. "I'm not going to squeal on you. Tell me what you do know."

"I'm sorry, Eldon."

"If that's the way it's going to be, *all right!*" and he turned on his heel and stormed out of the barn.

Roxie was in the kitchen helping her mother prepare breakfast when Eldon came to the door.

"What're you going to do this morning, Roxie?"

"I've got to help Mother. There are so many people around and everything."

"I thought maybe you'd go fishing with me," he said. "Everybody else around here is so busy, and I haven't even had a chance to find out whether there are any fish in the lake."

Roxie hesitated. "Mother has an awful lot to do."

"You go along this morning, dear," Mrs. Orlis broke in. "You've been working hard the last week or two. It'll do you good."

Eldon wanted to leave as soon as breakfast was over, but Roxie puttered around until Danny and the others had gone.

"Now," she said, getting into a light jacket, and taking the thermos she had filled with hot chocolate, "what kind of fish would you like to try for?"

"I thought we could go out and get a couple of muskies or big northerns this morning. And then go out for some walleyes this afternoon."

"I wish it were that simple," she said, smiling warmly.

Roxie got Ron's casting rod and tackle box, and checked the gas tank on the "Scappoose." Then she stepped back and glanced at the clouds on the western horizon.

"I didn't notice those before," she said hesitantly.

"They aren't so bad," Eldon answered. "There have been a lot heavier clouds than those since we've been up here, and we haven't had a storm yet."

"There are wind and rain both in those clouds. We can go out, but we don't want to get too far away."

"Something always happens whenever I want to do something," Eldon said. "It never fails."

Nevertheless, they got into the "Scappoose" and went over to Little McCoy.

"I'll row for a while," Roxie said, shutting off the motor. "You can cast."

He took the rod awkwardly and, using both hands, managed to throw the lure a dozen feet and make a tangled backlash. Roxie took the rod from him and untangled the line.

"I don't know why I ever let Dad talk me into coming up into this forsaken country anyway," he muttered. "It's been one huge bore ever since we left home."

She leaned forward on the oars and looked back at him.

"I know how you feel. But I can tell you how you can change all that, so you'll enjoy yourself wherever you go."

He looked at her suspiciously. "What kind of a line is this?"

"It isn't a line. It's the truth. I know from experience. The Bible tells us that the Lord Jesus came to live on earth and to die for you and me that we might have eternal life. If we confess our sin and put our trust in Him to save us, we'll begin to be happy and contented wherever we go."

"Humph!" he exclaimed. "Religion! That's all I need!"

"The Lord Jesus is the most important thing that any of us need," Roxie continued. " 'The fear of the Lord is clean,' the Bible tells us, 'enduring forever; the judgments of the Lord are true and righteous altogether. More to be desired are they than gold, yea, than much fine gold.' "

Eldon snorted his derision and cast clumsily toward shore. His casting rod arched.

"I've got one!" he shouted, jerking on the rod with both hands until rod and tip were almost double. "I've got one, Roxie!"

"Set the hook!"

"How do you do that?"

He had forgotten the reel had a handle and was pulling in desperation on the rod. Whatever was on the other end of the line, it didn't budge.

Roxie twisted around until she could see what was happening. There, leaning out over the water, was a scraggly evergreen! Eldon's lure was securely hooked in a tough branch an inch or two above the water.

"Oh, Eldon!" she exclaimed, trying to stifle her laughter. "All you've got is a tree!"

He eased the rod forward slowly. It straightened, except for a kink near the tip. His face was scarlet. For almost a minute he did not speak.

"If you say anything about this, Roxie Orbs," he said at last, "you'll be sorry!"

While they had been fishing and talking, Roxie had forgotten to watch the storm. Now, without warning, the wind lashed out of the west. She turned quickly to Eldon.

"We've got to head for home. It's going to rain in a couple of minutes."

"Is it safe for us to go across the bay?"

Roxie had turned to start the motor. She half stood in the boat and pointed. "Eldon!" she cried. "Look!"

"I don't see anything. Let's get back across the

bay before this storm gets any worse. We can't stay out here!"

"Look over that way!" she repeated. There, off the far point of Big McCoy Island, was an overturned boat! Two men were clinging to it!

CHAPTER 7

THE SECRET LEAKS OUT

The overturned boat was floundering helplessly in the water. For a brief instant Roxie could only see one of the men. She caught her breath sharply.

"We–We'd better get back across the bay," Eldon said stammering. "Those waves are getting higher all the time."

Roxie glanced back at him. Could it be possible that he still didn't see the boat and the men in the water, or was it fear that gripped him?

But there was no time to think of that now. She started the motor and edged the "Scappoose" expertly about. "Why are you heading that way?" her companion demanded. His voice was trembling and his swallow face had gone ashen.

"We've got to rescue those men!" she shouted above the roar of the wind.

"But we can't!" he protested in desperation. "We'll be drowned too!"

There was a prayer in Roxie's heart as she eased the throttle forward and guided the "Scappoose" out of the lea of Little McCoy Island, where the wind slammed towering waves at her prow. The little "Scappoose" reeled under the force of them, taking water and wallowing heavily. They weren't in too much danger now. "But when the desperate men in the water grabbed hold of the bouncing craft" – grimly she forced the thought from her mind.

There was only one thing that was important now. They had to get to those men quickly.

Rain began to dot the wind-torn water. It hit Roxie's cheeks. Eldon hunched his back against it.

"O God," she prayed inwardly, "help us to get there in time!"

It seemed to take so long, but it was probably no more than five minutes until they reached the overturned boat.

"We thought you'd never come!" one of the men gasped as he turned from their capsized boat and took hold of the "Scappoose."

"Don't try to climb into our boat," Roxie ordered. "Hang on to it and we'll take you to shore."

"We'd just about given up," the man said again.

"I was just telling Fred that I couldn't hang on much longer," Hank said weakly.

The two men clung to the stern of the "Scappoose" while Eldon rowed amateurishly to shore.

"I don't know how we can ever thank you enough," Hank said.

"The Lord must have caused me to look over this way," Roxie told them. "We were ready to leave when we noticed you."

"If you could take us across the bay to your place for the night," Hank suggested, "we'd be grateful to you. That old tub of ours isn't worth trying to rescue. The fact is, I don't think it could ever be made seaworthy again."

"If you don't think your folks would mind," Hank added.

"Oh, they wouldn't mind!" Roxie said. "In fact, they'd want me to bring you home."

They crossed the bay in the "Scappoose," cutting diagonally across to Pine Creek.

"When I saw you out there," Eldon said, "I told Roxie that we'd have to rescue you if we could. It's a good thing for you that I happened to be with her."

Roxie glanced at him but said nothing.

Her dad got some dry clothes for the two men and insisted that they stay with them at Angle Inlet until they got additional gear.

"We don't like to barge in on you this way," Fred Havens said. "You've already done so much for us."

"But we insist on it," Carl Orlis said graciously. "You can send in word with Cap for new gear and stay here until he brings it out on his next trip."

"We'd like to send for something for Roxie and this young man too," Hank Green added. "We will never be able to repay them."

"I was afraid that you were going to swamp the boat when we were trying to rescue you," Eldon said, smiling importantly. "But I managed to get you to shore all right."

The Orlis family accepted the two men without question, as they did everyone else who came to Angle Inlet. But Ron and Newton were somewhat suspicious.

"I'll tell you something, Ron," Newton said when they were getting ready for bed that night. "Those two guys act funny to me. They do not appear to be men who have almost lost their lives and have been deprived of several hundred dollars' worth of fishing and camping gear by reason of a storm. They do not seem upset enough, or thankful enough to have been spared."

"They do seem awfully calm."

"Indubitably! Indubitably! And besides, I'm not at all sure that I quite approve of their looks."

"I was thinking the same thing, Red. Maybe we ought to nose around a little tomorrow, over at American Point and Oak Island. Those fellows said they had been at both places."

"Capital, my true and brainy friend! Capital!"

The following morning Ron and Newton got up early, so they could make their trip and be back to Angle Inlet by the time the boat got in from Warroad.

"I can't figure out why those fellows would venture out in a storm that would upset their boat," Ron said as they went roaring down the lake toward American Point. "And why would they upset so close to shore? You'd think if they had been able to get that close to shore they'd have made it in under their own steam."

The boys stopped at American Point and at Oak Island, but learned only that the two men had outfitted at Oak Island and headed up the bay.

"Perhaps we are chasing wild geese on this detecting expedition," Newton said. "Everything those two men told us has been true, as far as we have been able to check."

Ron had just backed the "Scappoose" away from the Oak Island dock, and Newton was turning her around with the oars, when an elderly Indian came hobbling out and waved to them.

"There's Danny's old friend," Ron said, "Chief Rainy Weather."

"You ask about two white men?" the chief asked Ron. Ron nodded.

"I see," the old Indian said. "They over by Big McCoy Island with glasses – like this – " He made a gesture to indicate they had been using a pair of binoculars. "Then they get in boat and push it out in water. Crazy men." He shook his head. "They upset boat and yell and wave like everything! Crazy! Heap crazy!"

Ron thanked him warmly.

"Now, what do you make of that?" he asked when the chief had hobbled back to the Oak Island store.

"We were correct in our suspicions, Ronald. Absolutely correct. They must have done all this so they could be taken to your place."

"But I don't see why they would want to do that," Ron said, "or how they could have worked it if they did. How would they know that Roxie and Eldon were from our place? And why would they have picked that particular place?"

"The name 'Scappoose' is painted on the boat, isn't it?" Newton asked. "And Big and Little McCoy Islands are a favorite fishing location for your family and anyone who happens to be visiting. The chances are that someone from your place fishes out there at least every other day. The storm was just a bonus. They'd have attempted to pull this stunt regardless of the day. They watched Eldon and Roxie in the binoculars until they were almost positive they would be seen. Then they pulled their little trick."

"But why?"

"My dear Ronald, have you forgotten the film?"

"Do you suppose that's what they're after?"

"I'm positive."

"It does make sense," Ron agreed. "And coming to the folks this way, no one would suspect them. They've even got a perfect excuse for staying around for a while."

"What course do you think we ought to follow?" Newton asked.

"The first thing is to get hold of Danny and give him the scoop. Then we'll figure it out from there."

The two boys hurried back to Angle Inlet.

"I sure hope Danny's here," Ron said, cutting the motor and gliding up to the dock. "The sooner we can talk with him the better I'll like it."

But when they went up to the cabin, Mrs. Orlis already had dinner on the table.

"I'll fix you boys something in the kitchen in a few minutes," she said. "I would have waited for you, but Danny thought they ought to get some more pictures this afternoon, now that the storm is over."

"Oh, do you fellows take pictures?" Hank asked innocently. "I'm something of a camera enthusiast myself. What do you take, 35 mm slides?"

"Right now, we're shooting some 16 mm movie film," Danny answered.

"And you ought to see the film Danny's got," Eldon blurted. "You've never seen anything like it in your life."

Newton and Ron looked at him.

"Why?" Fred asked. "Is it any different than any other film?"

"Different?" Eldon echoed. "You ought to see it. It's the fastest color film you ever saw. It's as fast or faster than any black and white film that I've ever come across!"

Ron suddenly went numb. He looked over at Newton who was chewing his lower lip savagely.

The story was out! And there wasn't a thing they could do about it!

CHAPTER 8

"WHAT DO YOU HAVE?"

Silence settled over the little group at the table, a tense, uncomfortable silence. Danny looked quickly at his brother and Newton. Ron swallowed hard and began to cough. The color fled from Newton's face. His forehead moistened with perspiration and his eyes glazed. Everyone in the room was looking at him.

"So you have some new film," Fred Havens said. He tried to sound casual, but his voice was taut as whipcord. "That's interesting."

"Wait until you see what it'll do," Eldon went on. "Your eyes'll really pop!"

"Now you've got me curious."

"Ronald," Newton broke in suddenly, and in a loud voice, "do you suppose anyone would like to join us in an effort to hook a worthy piscatorial adversary?"

"He means, 'Would anyone like to go fishing?' " Ron translated, equally loud. "The walleyes really ought to be on a rampage today. Anybody like to go with us?"

But it was almost as though they hadn't even spoken.

"Now you've got me curious," Fred repeated. "What is this film, young man?"

"Humph," Eldon snorted. "They won't let me know a thing. But they can't fool me. They've got the best color film you ever saw."

Hank turned to Danny. "I'm interested in film too, in a minor way. What do you have, something from one of the big companies?"

"We're only starting to use it," Danny answered guardedly. "We don't know too much about it yet."

Fred moved his chair closer to him. "If it isn't asking too much, could we see some of the pictures you've taken?"

"I was just thinking the same thing," Hank put in.

"I'm sure you wouldn't be interested in seeing the film," Danny told them. "A lot of editing has to be done and the sound has to be dubbed in. It really isn't in shape to show."

"But that wouldn't matter to us at all."

The two men continued to press him, but Danny changed the subject.

"Now," Ron exclaimed, "would anybody like to go fishing?"

But no one was interested in fishing. The two men spoke of the film again, but Danny refused to hear them. They were still sitting at the table when the boat from Warroad came in.

"Hurry and clear the table, Roxie," Mrs. Orlis said. "Here come the boys from the Fisheries' boat with a couple of passengers. And they haven't had dinner."

Everyone got up from the table and began to file outside.

"Danny," Ron whispered to his brother at the first opportunity, "we've got to talk to you."

He nodded, almost imperceptibly. He followed along behind the others and waited until the boat was secure. Then he sauntered off behind the cabins. Ron and Newton followed.

"We are in desperate straits, Daniel," Newton whispered, his voice tense. "The situation calls for action – and quickly. Those men aren't stranded here. This is some sort of an ugly game."

Hurriedly, Ron told him what they had learned.

"That fits," Danny said when he finished. "That fits very neatly."

"But what are we going to do?" Ron asked. "Every minute we stay here gives those fellows that much more of a chance to steal the film."

"I'll talk to Gil," Danny said after a time. "If we can keep mum about the location of our camp site and get out of here right away, we ought to be able to give them the slip."

"But what if Mr. Pemberton doesn't want to leave now?" Ron asked. "He's still got some shots to take around here."

"You must be persuasive, Daniel," Newton said tensely.

"We have to get out of here at once."

Danny talked with Mr. Pemberton later in the afternoon and convinced him that they ought to leave at once for the camp in Ontario north of Kenora.

"I had to tell Gil a little more than he knew already," Danny said to Newton and Ron, "but he didn't ask many questions, and he doesn't know enough to cause any trouble."

"At the moment, I am scarcely concerned about Mr. Pemberton at all," Newton replied.

"We'll radio for Tex to come and take us up to the campsite in his plane," Danny continued. "The Pembertons will follow in theirs."

"You'd better put that film in a good place, Red," Ron said seriously. "Now that those guys know we've got it, there's no telling what they'll do."

If the two men were actually interested in the film, they gave no sign of it during the rest of the day. They went to their cabin after the mail was distributed and slept for a couple of hours. Then they went out on the dock and talked with the captain of the Fisheries' boat about bringing up some more supplies from Warroad for them, in addition to what Cap was getting.

"We can't stay around here taking advantage of your hospitality any longer, Mr. Orlis," Hank told Carl with an obvious effort to be friendly. "We've already been here much too long."

"Our doors are always open to those who are in trouble."

"I know, but we're not going to take advantage of you any longer. As soon as we get our things from Warroad, we'll be on our way."

The following morning Danny asked his dad to take the two men somewhere fishing while Tex came in and got them.

"Take them over on Harrison Creek, or up the Bear River," the boy suggested, "so they won't see the plane take off and land."

"What's this all about, Danny?"

"I can't tell you, Dad, but it's awfully important. Tex will be in for us about eight, so you'll have to take them early in the morning."

"You leave that to me. Of course, when they come back and find that you're gone they're going to ask questions."

That evening Carl Orlis started talking about the wonderful fishing as they sat around in the living room. And in a few minutes Fred and Hank were suggesting that they go out the next morning.

"Fine," Mr. Orlis said, smiling. "I've been wanting to go fishing for a couple of weeks. But I want to go early. Do you think you fellows can be ready to leave here by six?"

"Can we?" Fred echoed, looking at his companion.

Mr. Orlis and Hank and Fred had been gone for almost two hours when Tex touched down to pick up Danny and Ron and Newton.

"We'll only take part of the gear this trip," the pilot

said. "I'll take you fellows up and leave you while I come back for the rest."

"Fine. Gil Pemberton can follow us the first trip."

They loaded the little planes to capacity.

"I–I don't know what to think about going into any wilder country than this," Eldon said uneasily, as they all stood together on the bank of the little creek before taking off. "This is the end of the world as far as I'm concerned."

"If you think this is wild," Ron said brightly, "you ought to see the country where we're going. It'll make Angle Inlet seem like New York City on a Saturday night."

Newton grinned.

"Indubitably, Ronald! Indubitably!"

They stopped at the Canadian Customs office near Oak Island and got clearance, then headed straight for the wilderness north of Kenora. Ron looked intently out the window of the little plane. The land that lay below them was a maze of lakes and muskeg and rivers – lakes that had probably never been fished more than two or three times in the last twenty years. Lakes with record trout and muskies and tackle-busting northerns. Lakes with walleyes that had never seen a lure.

"Danny," Ron said hopefully, "do you suppose we'll have time to do some fishing while we're up here?"

"I didn't bring my tackle along for the ride," Danny answered. "We'll have to see if these lakes are all that Dad says they are."

"How you can center your cogitation upon anything so mundane as enticing a fish to strike at a piece of metal, when matters of tremendous proportions are hanging in the balance, is beyond me," Newton said nervously. "Right now, I am directing all my attention toward getting this film exposed and returned to Dr. Desmond before those desperadoes relieve us of it."

"I just thought of something, Danny," Ron said, a smile lurking at the corners of his mouth. "The best way I know to keep Hank and Fred from getting our film is to have Red go back and tell them how the stuff works. While they're trying to figure out what he's talking about, we can have the film taken and get it back to Dr. Desmond."

"I think you've got something there."

But Newton's face was serious. "Those two nefarious individuals are going to cause us a large measure of trouble. *I know it!*"

CHAPTER 9

IN MOOSE COUNTRY

Tex Williams consulted his map and nosed downward.

"We're about there, Danny. See anything that looks familiar?"

Danny squinted down at the islands. "We left a piece of cloth on the rocks for a marker. If we can–" He pointed suddenly. "There it is!"

"Right you are! Tex circled and landed in front of the little island.

By the time they had taxied to the island, Gil Pemberton dropped down. He climbed out of his two-place Piper Cub and looked about approvingly.

"You picked a good place for a camp, Danny," he said. "And there ought to be a lot of things to photograph here." Eldon climbed out of the plane and made his way to shore.

"Do you mean we're going to have to stay in this

sleazy dump for a couple of weeks?" he demanded of no one in particular. "I think I'll go back to Angle Inlet with Tex."

"I think you'll stay here with the rest of us," his dad said sharply.

The boy's lower lip curled. "You can make me stay, but you can't make me like it."

They unlashed the canoes that had been secured to the fuselage of each plane, and got their gear ashore.

"Think you've got enough grub to last for a couple of days, Danny?" Tex asked when he was ready to take off. "I might have a charter trip or two I could take, if I thought you fellows wouldn't need the rest of your outfit right off."

Danny checked the boxes of film. "I think we've got enough film to last for a week," he said, "depending on how fast we shoot it, and I know we've got enough food for that long. I don't think you'll have to come right back unless things work out that way."

"I'll see you before you run out of grub." Then Tex climbed into the plane and started the motor.

"Wish I were going with him," Eldon muttered under his breath.

Gil and Danny had each grabbed an armload and started up the gentle slope.

"You fellows had better get a move on," Danny called. "We've got a lot to do to get camp ready before night."

"I don't care if it never gets ready."

Ron looked at Eldon and grinned. "If it rains, you'll be sorry you ever said that."

Ron and Newton set to work together, cutting tent poles and stakes, and ditching each tent after pitching it. Eldon made a half-hearted effort to help, grumbling his disgust.

"Now that those tents are up," Newton said, I must find a suitable location for my special tent." He walked about the camp site, studying it carefully.

"What's the matter with you, Red?" Ron demanded.

"Aren't you going to be sociable and stay with the rest of us?"

"I think you should know by this time, Ronald," Newton began, "that I am exceedingly particular about the quality of my neighbors and associates. Unfortunately, circumstances make it impossible for me to get too far away from you–"

"Circumstances like – you get hungry and have to have something to eat, or you're afraid you'll get lost in the woods," Ron answered laughing.

But Eldon glared at Newton. "I don't think you're such a prize, Red."

Newton's expression did not change. "I am quite aware of that, Eldon," he said, "but please don't let it get back to my mother. She likes me." He drew himself up a bit. "And the name is not Red. It is Newton Jonathan Edward Bostwick III, named after the jolly chap who let the apple conk him on the head."

The others laughed, but Eldon stormed down to the water's edge and looked out across the lake.

Ron and Newton selected a spot away from the other tents, where the shade was deepest, and set up the small, dark umbrella tent Newton had brought along.

"What's this tent for?" Ron whispered. "And why such a heavy one? You don't need anything like this up here."

"That is where you are mistaken," the young scientist informed him. "This tent is to serve as my laboratory."

"Your what?" Ron's eyes widened.

"Dark room to you, Ronald, old top. It happens to be a special tent that Dr. Desmond and I developed. A regular tent lined with high-grade oilcloth. It is absolutely, and positively, light proof."

Ron pursed his lips.

"Don't you think it should have been pitched closer to the other tents?" he asked. "Way off by itself this way it's bound to invite a lot of questions."

"From whom?" Newton asked. "The chipmunks, or the partridge, or do you think a black bear is apt to get his curiosity aroused?"

"You can scoff if you want to," Ron countered, "but there are people back here, even though we are in the wilderness. There are prospectors and game wardens and Indians, and even a fisherman now and then."

Newton looked about. "You make it sound as though I've pitched my tent in Central Station."

"Why don't we talk to Danny and see what he says?"

"Yes," Danny said, "there are a few people who get up here. Take this lake, for example. It's undoubtedly been fished five or six times in the past 20 years. And I suppose an Indian goes through here every year or so."

"Then I take it your considered judgment would be that the danger is slight."

"Slight is the word for it," Danny replied.

It took most of the afternoon for the little party to pitch their tents and arrange the camp. Danny put Gil and Eldon to hauling firewood, while he took short lengths of rope and suspended the duffle bags and knapsacks from the limbs of trees.

"Christmas in June," Newton observed sagely, "and Danny is already decorating his tree."

"I learned about this the hard way," Danny explained. "The first time you have to go hungry for a day or two, because a bear has helped himself to your grub, you'll remember to put it up where he isn't so apt to be tempted."

"Bears!" Eldon snorted. "I haven't seen a decent-sized animal since we've been up here. We probably won't photograph anything bigger than a jack rabbit."

"Our jack rabbits happen to be snowshoes," Ron informed him.

After supper Danny got out his Bible.

"Not that again!" Eldon moaned aloud. "I thought we left that religion back at Angle Inlet."

"We can't pick up the Lord Jesus or put Him aside that easily." Danny said. "We must come face to face with Him and either take Him as our Savior or reject Him. Once we take a stand as Christian, He expects us to live like Christians. In other words, being a Christian is a 24-hour-a-day business, seven days a week."

"I can assure you, Eldon," Newton put in seriously "that what Daniel tells you is true. Just a year ago I had the same opinion, exactly, of the Lord Jesus and anything that had to do with Him. But I soon learned that Daniel and Ronald had something I didn't have. Something that I had to have if I were going to live a happy, well-ordered, satisfying life."

"And so, you became a Christian, or a religious fanatic, or whatever you call it," Eldon countered, "and immediately every problem you ever had was solved."

"Not at all. Quite the contrary. It seemed to me that I had more problems, if that were possible. But God did all that He promises to do. He has given me the strength to face my problems, whatever comes."

Eldon did not answer. He had gotten to his feet when Danny was talking. Now he quietly sat down again and listened while Danny read from the Word of God and prayed. The rest of the evening he said very little.

"What do you plan for tomorrow?" Gil Pemberton asked Danny before turning in.

"I thought maybe we ought to scout around a little and see if we can find a moose."

Gil Pemberton consulted his notes. "You can suit yourself, Danny. But we won't need moose pictures for some time. They don't come into the film until quite late. I'd just as soon get some of these other things out of the way first."

"We'd better take our moose pictures when we can get them," Danny answered. "That's probably going to be our toughest assignment. That and to get pictures of an old bear with her cubs. I thought we ought to do a little looking for those two scenes right along."

Gil nodded his approval.

Eldon stuck out his head from his tent. "I don't know what you're planning for tomorrow, but you can count me out. I'm not getting up in the middle of the night to traipse around among the mosquitoes looking for any kind of an animal."

Ron and Newton were already in their sleeping bags. "Danny says we ought to make friends with Eldon," Ron said softly, "and show that we like him."

"That is the Christian way," Newton answered, "but to me it appears to be exceedingly difficult."

"The guy acts like he wants people to hate him. I can't figure him out at all."

"Nor can I. We must remember to pray for him, Ronald."

"That's the only thing that'll do him any good," Ron said sleepily. "The trouble is that he doesn't know the Lord Jesus as his Savior."

The next morning Eldon came straggling out for breakfast just as the others were finishing.

"What's the matter? Didn't you fix any bacon for me?" he demanded.

"Breakfast is over," Danny told him pleasantly. "But you can get some bacon out of my knapsack, and the duffle bag next to it has some eggs in it."

"But it's not my turn to cook," Eldon complained. "I had to cook for everybody. I don't see why Ron doesn't."

"We have one breakfast, Eldon," his dad said, in a stern voice. "If you had gotten up earlier you could have had Ron fix you something. Now you'll have to fix your own or go without."

Eldon continued to grumble, but he got the bacon and cut a couple of thick slices.

"Going out with us this morning?" Ron asked when they were ready to go.

Eldon did not answer.

Ron and Newton went off in one canoe, and Gil and Danny in the other.

"Now, just where do you plan to look for a moose?" Newton asked.

"A moose is wherever you happen to find him," Ron said gaily. "It's just as easy to hunt for a moose here from the lake, as it is to tramp through the muskeg."

They paddled among the islands and up one small stream after another, searching for some sign of a moose.

"I am afraid we are going to have to inform Daniel that the moose have departed without a trace," Newton said when they finally headed back toward camp. "If there were any moose in the territory we would have seen them."

Back at camp for their noon meal, they discovered that Danny and Gil had not found any moose tracks either.

"We can give it up for the rest of the day," Danny said, "and try again tomorrow. I've been thinking of some fishing shots, Gil. How does that sound to you?"

"Do you mean I get to do the fishing?" Mr. Pemberton asked, smiling.

"Ron and I volunteer," Newton said, "and so does Eldon, if he wants to go along."

"Fishing?" the latter echoed, wrinkling his nose. "That's for the birds."

Nevertheless, at the last moment he got into the canoe with them.

"Sure glad you changed your mind," Ron told him pleasantly. "I don't think there's a better fishing lake in Ontario. You should have seen the fish Danny and Tex brought back the day they came up here to find a campsite."

"Fishing's for the birds," Eldon said, contempt in his voice, "but at least it's something to do."

Ron took the fishing gear in his canoe, and Danny and Gil Pemberton had the camera.

"Now all you fellows have to do is catch a 15- or 20-pound northern," Danny said as they shoved off. "One that will do a lot of jumping and walking on his tail, so we can get some good action pictures."

"Is it all right if I catch him?" Ron asked in mock sincerity, "or should I let Eldon or Red have the honor?"

Newton fastened a Lazy Ike to his leader and began to cast. His first throw produced a savage strike that almost jerked the rod from his hand.

"I've got one!" he shouted. "I've–" He stopped miserably. "He's gone!"

"Why didn't you hang on to him?" Danny demanded. "We can't take pictures unless you catch some fish."

"I would have," Newton answered. "That was certainly my most firm intention. However, I glanced your way and perceived that you did not yet have your camera in hand. So I decided to wait until you were ready."

"I feel as though I didn't go to school at all when I hear that boy talk," Gil Pemberton said softly to Danny.

Newton made ready to cast again.

It was then that Ron saw the moose! They had rounded a little point of ground so Newton could work the lily pads on the other side. There, in water up to his shoulders, stood a moose!

For a moment Ron froze. The big animal was so busy feeding that he hadn't even heard them.

"Danny!" Ron whispered tensely. "Don't make a noise, but look around."

Danny moaned. "Of all the dumb tricks! I came off without any film!"

"I told you what kind of a photographer he was, Dad," Eldon said triumphantly. "I told you."

"By a queer coincidence," Newton began, smirking good-naturedly, "it so happens that I have in my possession a second camera." He reached behind him and out of a battered canvas bag brought a camera exactly like Danny's. "And I have wisely made certain that it is loaded with film."

"Cut the bragging, Red," Ron whispered, "and let's get with it! That old boy isn't going to stay here all day."

"Truly said," Newton answered. "However, I just wanted to call attention to the fact that I am adequately prepared. I am afraid that I am not entirely appreciated about this locality."

"You're going to have to walk back to our camp from this locality," Ron told him, "if you don't can the chatter and get that camera unlimbered."

Ron began to paddle silently toward the feeding moose.

"You aren't going any closer to that–that beast, are you?" Eldon asked uncertainly.

"We most assuredly are going to move close enough to expose some film," Newton told him. "That, my dear Eldon, is why we came up here."

"Take me over to shore and let me out first."

"All you've got to do, Eldon," Ron whispered, "is stay in the canoe and keep the moose outside. If you do that, he won't hurt you at all."

Quietly, Ron pushed the aluminum canoe forward. Newton's body tensed as he squinted into the viewfinder.

"Getting better, Ronald. But it would be still better if you could transport me a little closer."

Eldon, who was sitting in the prow, began to squirm.

The moose didn't know they were within a hundred miles. His great, ugly head would go down and stay for what seemed to be a long time but was probably only a minute or two. Then he would throw it high and stand motionless, chewing.

"Are you getting any pictures?" Ron whispered.

For answer Newton started the camera again. He had taken a few feet of film without bothering the animal, but they were within 15 feet of him now. The instant the shutter began to whir the moose's head went up, ears twitching, and his nostrils testing the wind. His eyes were wide.

"Ron!" Danny shouted in warning. "Get out of there!"

The sound of Danny's voice was the trigger that released the coiled spring in the huge moose's body. At that very instant the animal snorted with rage and lunged forward, his antlers lowering!

CHAPTER 10

AN ANGRY MOOSE

That beast is after us!" Eldon shrieked. He turned in sudden desperation and tried to climb over Newton. "Let me out of here!"

The moose lunged with his great antlers, just missing the prow. He stumbled clumsily and almost lost his balance, but only for an instant, the blink of an eyelash. He got his feet solidly under him again and went plunging after them.

"Paddle, Ron!" Newton cried.

"That's what I'm doing," Ron answered between gritted teeth.

He was paddling backward frantically. The light canoe seemed to skim over the water, but he was able to keep only a scant yard or so out of the infuriated animal's reach.

Eldon was still trying to climb over Newton to get a little farther away from the moose. The canoe tipped dangerously.

"Sit down, Eldon!" Newton ordered, clinging to his camera and his position in the canoe.

"You'd just as well sit down and relax," Ron said laughing. "You don't need to worry about that moose getting into our canoe. We don't have room for him!"

"Very funny!" Eldon exclaimed. "I'm about to *die* laughing!"

"And all the while I thought it was the moose who was going to cause your untimely end," Newton said.

"He's going to sink us!"

Newton had been taking pictures all the while.

"That old gentleman seems to be perturbed about something, Ronald," he said casually as though he had been talking about a man across the street. "And the distance between the end of our canoe and his horns is getting shorter. I would strongly suggest that you expend every effort to paddle faster and–"

He choked off as the moose threw himself forward, just nicking the aluminum prow. He only caught it with the tip of his horns, but it was enough to throw them violently.

"Paddle, Ron!" Newton shouted. "Paddle!"

Eldon was sitting there, eyes bugged. He had grasped the gunwales with his hands, and the perspiration stood out on his forehead. His mouth moved, but no words came.

"Keeping going, Ron!" Danny shouted. "He's almost in deep water!"

Even as he spoke the moose began to swim. He kept after them, but now Ron could easily outdistance him.

"You are now beginning to draw away from him, Ronald," Newton said. "Slow down slightly until I finish shooting this film."

"Don't pay any attention to him," Eldon said, gasping.

For almost a hundred yards the angered moose followed after them. Ron slowed down until he was only a canoe length behind.

"Now," Newton said at last, putting his camera aside, "we can outdistance Mr. Moose at your leisure."

"It's about time," Eldon said thankfully.

Ron turned and headed out toward the open lake. The moose followed along behind for another 75 yards or so, and then turned back reluctantly.

Ron lay the paddle across the gunwales and leaned forward on it.

"That is what I would call a realistic bit of film," Newton said. "And fortunately the photographer was of sufficient ability to assure us a most outstanding bit of photography."

Ron grinned wearily. "But for a minute or two, I didn't know whether we were going to have a canoe or not. That old boy was close!"

"That is the understatement of the year." Newton turned back to face Eldon. "By the way, where did you think you were going a couple of minutes ago?" His eyes were twinkling.

"You wouldn't have been so brave either, if you'd been looking into that moose's eyes the way I did.

Besides, I was the closest to him. I'm the one he would have grabbed first."

Newton would have answered him, but Danny and Gil Pemberton paddled up just then.

"Would you fellows like to go through that one again," Danny asked, "or do you think you got a good take?"

"It's good," Ron said quickly. "In fact, it's perfect. Couldn't be better!"

"And besides," Newton broke in, "we have developed a sudden allergy to all species of moose."

"You guys can laugh if you want to," Eldon exclaimed, "but that wasn't anything to laugh about. It was close, I tell you!"

They were paddling back toward the camp site.

"Yes, sir," Newton continued as they got out of the canoes and went up to the tents. "There is one thing we must give Eldon credit for. He can move with considerable alacrity. I thought you were going to run and jump into the canoe with your dad and Danny. For a fact."

Eldon was coloring slightly.

"Lay off, will you?"

"You just aren't aware of how comical you appeared to us," Newton said snickering. "If Daniel had had his camera available, we'd have had the best comedy scene of the film!"

Eldon glared at him but said nothing.

It was Danny's turn to cook that evening. As he

busied himself over the stove, Newton went into the tent where he did the developing.

"How about a swim, Eldon?" Ron asked. "There's a swell place to dive off the rocks."

Eldon shook his head.

"I can think of a lot of things that are more fun." He glanced around. "Where's Newton?"

"He's fiddling with his film, but he ought to have it developed by this time." He turned to face the tent. "Hey, Red," he called loudly, "are you about done in there? I want to go for a swim?"

"Take it easy," Newton answered. "I can be with you in a short time."

Ron went down by the lake and sat on a big rock. It was hard to understand a guy like Eldon. He always acted as though he didn't care about anything or anyone. And he couldn't let anyone know that he was enjoying himself. Ron sighed deeply.

At that moment Newton let out a yell.

"Shut that canvas!" he shouted. "I've got this film out!"
"I was just trying to see what you're doing," Eldon said.

Ron turned in time to see a queer little smirk on the boy's face.

"Don't do that!" Danny and Gil Pemberton cried out.

But they were too late. Eldon had finally managed to open the inner oil-cloth door, allowing a narrow shaft of light to stream in.

"Now you've done it!" Newton exclaimed. "The whole reel of film is ruined!"

By this time, the others had run to the tent.

"You've been around film enough to know that you can't do a thing like that, Eldon," his dad said sternly. "What's the matter with you anyway?"

"I just wanted to see what he was doing," the boy stammered defensively. "I didn't mean to hurt anything. I just wanted to see how he developed this new film."

Danny shoved past the others and went in where Newton was. "Did he spoil the film we just took, Newton?" he asked.

The boy shook his head. "No, I already had that in the fix. It's all right. But I had this reel out and was loading the magazines for tomorrow. I'm afraid the whole batch of film is ruined!"

"That's bad. Is there any way we can tell?"

"Not here. The only thing we could do is use it and see how much of it developed."

"We wouldn't dare do that," Danny answered. "There's too much risk involved to take a chance of having our best shots ruined. We won't be able to use it at all."

He went back to the stove. "There's nothing we can do about it."

Gil Pemberton followed him.

"I guess you know how sorry I am," he said softly. "I don't know why Eldon would do a thing like that. He's been out with me on dozens of jobs."

Danny smiled reassuringly. "When the Lord Jesus gets hold of him, Gil, you won't have to worry about this sort of thing happening. His entire life will change."

Gil Pemberton looked at Danny almost wistfully. "I'm beginning to think that nothing will make him change."

When they had finished eating, Danny called Newton and Ron aside. "How much film do we have left, Newton?"

"There are two more 200-foot rolls. But we've been using a lot of film. At the rate we've been going I doubt whether it'll last more than three or four days."

"Dr. Desmond was going to ship some more, wasn't he?"

"He informed me that he would endeavor to estimate our needs and to keep us well supplied," Newton answered. "It is reasonable to assume that another shipment should reach Angle Inlet about the time we expose the last of our stock."

"Good! Gil and I will go back after it when we shoot up what we have."

"And leave us up here with that Eldon?" Ron demanded.

"I'd like to talk with you guys about Eldon," Danny went on. "He's got a terrible chip on his shoulder, and no sense of humor at all. Why don't you ease up on him a little?"

"I didn't think we had been so rough on him," Ron answered.

"With him you're going to have to be extra careful." Danny glanced over his shoulder and lowered his voice a little. "That's why this affair happened tonight. He got mad because you had been razzing him a bit, and he decided to get back at you."

Newton nodded. "I perceived the same thing, Daniel, and I regret it exceedingly. It was my clumsy jesting that caused the trouble."

Danny rumpled Newton's thick, red hair.

"Just be easy on him, fellows, and keep praying for him. What he really needs is the Lord Jesus in complete control of his life."

CHAPTER 11

"THAT'S THEM!"

The work went very well the next two or three days. Danny found tracks that indicated bear and fox and muskrat were in the immediate area, and he and Gil Pemberton shot some more scenes of a beaver colony.

"We ought to wrap this up before long," Danny said to his brother and Newton during one of their infrequent talks alone. "If things go the way they have been, we'll have the film wrapped up and ready for delivery before long."

"That is the most gratifying news you have divulged since we came up here." Newton took a deep breath. "This film is going to mean success for Dr. Desmond and an opportunity to build the sort of laboratory he needs to carry on his research. News that we have finished will be most pleasing to him. He will assist you in the editing, if you wish, and make you a print for the Canadian Tourist Bureau. And then he will collect his award."

"You know," Ron said when Newton finished, "I don't believe Hank and Fred ever did find out where we are. We haven't seen anything of them, and they've had more than enough time to get up here."

"We could have been imagining things when we suspected them," Danny went on. "Maybe they weren't interested in your film at all, Newton."

"That, Daniel, is extremely doubtful," Newton countered. "We were much too clever for them. That is why they were unable to follow us."

"They aren't up here," Ron said thankfully. "That's the main thing."

As the days passed, the expedition continued to go smoothly. Even Eldon acted a little more friendly, as he and Newton and Ron helped Danny and his dad.

"The thing I can't figure out," he said one afternoon as they sat down to rest on a little knoll, "is how Danny expects us to locate a doe and her fawn by tracks. And he said he wanted a *young* doe."

"It's really easy when you know how," Ron told him.

"That I'll believe when I see it."

"No, it's the truth," Ron went on. "The tracks of any animal are just like a sign. All you have to do is to be able to read them."

He got up and began to move cautiously up the narrow island trail. A moment or two later he paused and pointed to the dainty little tracks in the soft ground. "Now this is the track of a doe."

Eldon looked at him suspiciously. "What makes you say that?"

Before answering, Ron followed the tracks a few steps, studying them carefully.

"They're doe tracks, all right. See how small they are? A buck's track would be half again as large. And they point straight ahead, while a buck's tracks toe out."

Eldon shook his head. "I don't get it. I don't get it at all."

"If you'll look around on either side of the trail, I'm sure we'll find the tracks of a fawn. Most does have fawns at this time of year."

Eldon went on one side while Newton went on the other. A moment later the young scientist called out, "I've found something over here. Better come and investigate, Ronald."

"She's got a fawn, all right." Ron turned to Eldon. "Now are you convinced that we've found the tracks of a doe?"

"I guess so," he said grudgingly, "but I still don't see how you can do it."

Ron continued to examine the tracks. "Just as I thought, something startled our doe and she took off in a big hurry."

"Now wait a minute. Wait a minute. That I don't swallow." Eldon's temper began to rise. "I may not know much about the woods, but I'm not that gullible."

"Ronald is telling us the truth."

"You'd stick up for him, no matter what he said."

Ron began to grin. "And I can tell you something else about our doe," he said. "She's young."

Eldon snorted in disbelief.

"All right, I'll show you. First of all, we know she's a young deer because the tracks of her hind feet are ahead of the front feet." He pointed to the tracks the hard-running deer had made. Her tracks were sharply etched in the soft ground.

"This is the sort of track a young deer makes," Ron explained. "Her stride is so long that her hind feet come up ahead of the place where her front feet were. All that is showing of her front tracks are these little half-moons, and they're at the back of her rear tracks."

"But if she is old," Newton asked, "what then?"

"The tracks are reversed. These little half-moons are in front of the rear tracks, which means that she isn't as spry as she used to be. Make sense?"

"Indubitably, Ronald! Indubitably!"

"At the moment we had better forego our lesson in tracks and woodlore," Newton said, "and go back for Daniel and Mr. Pemberton. They would be exceedingly unhappy if they missed an opportunity to photograph a deer and her fawn."

Eldon was surprised that it took Danny and his father only a couple of hours to track down the doe and her still-spotted fawn.

The two of them crept forward cautiously until they spied them, lying peacefully on a grassy hillside a short distance ahead.

"That's a beautiful picture, Orlis," Gil Pemberton whispered, his voice tense. "We ought to get as much footage here as we possibly can. People will love this scene."

Danny had been rationing his film, trying to make it last as long as possible. But he couldn't spare film in an opportunity like this. Both the doe and her fawn were out in a little clearing, upwind, so they didn't even know that the men were about.

The fawn danced daintily across the grass as though she were posing for them. The doe grazed for a while, and watched the fawn as she leaped and danced gracefully. All the while Danny was clipping off the film.

Finally, he turned to Gil. "I guess this is the end of that. I've shot up the last of it."

"Isn't there any more at camp?"

Danny shook his head.

"I stuck the last of it in my pocket when we came out here this afternoon."

Gil sighed wearily. "That means we've got to go back to Angle Inlet."

"The film ought to be there," Danny answered. "Newton said we would be getting regular shipments. We can fly down in the morning, and if it's there we ought to be back by noon."

Newton developed the footage they took that day and Danny put it in the plane.

The following morning, he was up when the first gray streaks of dawn were at work chasing away the gloom of night. By the time the others got up and were dressed, he had breakfast ready.

"We'll be back as quickly as we can, Ron," he explained. "Surely the film will be there today or tomorrow."

"You mean you're going to leave us up here alone?" Eldon echoed. "Without either Dad or Danny?"

"We've got plenty to eat," Ron told him. "There isn't a thing to worry about. We'll get along."

"We'll get along," the other boy said petulantly, "if we don't die of boredom. That's the trouble with this place. There's not a thing to do. I don't see how anyone can stand to be in a place like this."

Nobody answered him.

Danny and Gil took off into the wind. The boys watched until they disappeared over the trees.

"You know, Ronald," Newton said, lowering his voice, "I too am somewhat concerned about being up here without Daniel and Mr. Pemberton."

Ron nodded.

"I'll feel better myself when they get back."

While the boys were waiting for the dishwater to heat, Ron took a small, deerskin envelope from a pocket of his jacket. It was fastened securely with an inner-tube band.

Eldon had gone off to one side and was sitting on a huge rock. Although he tried to act as though he didn't care what Newton and Ron did, he kept eying the latter. Ron opened the packet to remove his Bible. Newton checked the water on the stove and sat down beside his friend.

"Why don't you read a chapter or two while we're waiting?"

Ron thumbed through the Bible.

"What shall I read?"

"Danny was reading 1 Corinthians 12 last night," Newton said. "Why don't you read chapter 13?"

As Ron began to read of love and how important it is, Eldon sauntered over to them and sat down. When the reading was finished, Eldon said belligerently, "Now that's a lot of malarkey."

Ron looked up.

"What do you mean?"

"All that rot about love being so all-fired important," Eldon continued. "It's words. That's all it is. Just words. A fellow can get along without love just as he can get along without anything else."

"But you can't get along without love," Ron said. "Love is the most important thing in the world. It was because of love that God sent the Lord Jesus down to earth. It was because He loved us that He died on the cross for us...."

A strange, haunted look came into Eldon's eyes. For a moment he looked at Ron with desperate longing. Then he got to his feet and hurried away.

Ron and Newton sat for a long while without speaking. Finally, Newton turned to the boy.

"I can see now what Danny was trying to inform us about. Eldon is miserable, unhappy, and lonely."

"And the Lord Jesus is the only One who can do anything about it," Ron added.

Together they bowed their heads and prayed.

It was not until after they had finished the dishes and put everything away that Eldon came sauntering back to join them.

"Sunday school over?"

The boys did not answer him.

"We're about ready to go fishing," Newton told him. "I would like to sink my teeth into some good, thick walleye steaks."

"If we can catch any."

"We'll catch them. I'm not worried about that!"

Eldon was in the center of the canoe, as usual, when they went out fishing. Ron and Newton were at the paddles. They made their way around the corner of the little island where they were camped and headed for the far shore of the lake.

"Why are we going way over there to fish?" Eldon asked.

"Fishing is always better on the other side of the lake," Newton informed him, smiling. "Weren't you aware of that?"

As they spoke Ron looked up – just in time to catch a glimpse of another canoe poking its nose around the end of an island a mile or so away.

"Red! Eldon!" he whispered, voice tense. "Look over there!"

"What is it?" Eldon asked. "I don't see anything except another canoe with a couple of men in it!"

"That's them!" Newton exclaimed. "That's Hank and Fred!"

"Are you sure?"

"I'd recognize them anywhere!"

CHAPTER 12

A LOUD ROAR!

The men in the other canoe were paddling leisurely, the way fishermen do.

"Are you sure it's Hank and Fred?" Ron managed, crouching slightly, as though that would help keep him from being seen.

"Positive!"

Eldon stared at them disdainfully. "What's the matter with you guys, anyway?" he demanded. "Hank and Fred are all right. There isn't anything to be so scared about."

"That," Newton said, lowering his voice, "is a matter of considerable conjecture."

"You guys make me laugh! And you were the ones who razzed me because I happened to be uneasy about that moose. And you're scared to death of a couple of ordinary fellows!"

By this time Newton was able to move again. He thrust his paddle savagely into the water. "Ronald, I have come to the conclusion that we ought to depart as quickly as possible."

"That's the best thing you've said all day."

They both paddled rapidly until the island was between them and the two men.

"There!" Ron exclaimed, sighing his relief. "They can't see us now."

"If, indeed, they haven't already observed us," Newton said.

"Do you think they have?" Ron asked.

"Now listen!" Eldon broke in. "What's this all about? Why does it make so much difference if they have seen us?"

Ron and Newton acted as though they had not heard.

"How do you suppose they found out where we are?" Ron asked.

"They could not have traced us," Newton said, "and I'm positive that no one gave them the information."

"I have it! Tex filed a flight plan at the airport before he took off from Baudette. He always does that as a safety measure."

Newton's mouth narrowed. "That could account for it. Such records probably aren't kept too secret. Anyone giving a plausible excuse could have access to them."

"That doesn't make any difference now," Ron said, glancing about nervously. "What we've got to do is get out of here. If Hank and Fred did see us, they'll be heading over this way to investigate."

"It would be most prudent of us, Ronald," Newton told him, turning the canoe expertly with a paddle, "to go around a few islands, in case they are following us, and confuse them thoroughly."

"I want to know what's going on around here," Eldon broke in irritably. "I'm out here with you guys. I've got a right to know what's going on!"

"Right now," Newton said, "the only thing 'going on,' as you put it, is a lot of hard paddling."

"And there's got to be a lot more of it before we get back to camp," Ron added.

The sweat stood out on Ron's forehead and his arms and shoulders ached as they paddled. But he did not miss a stroke, and neither did Newton. They took a long, circuitous route around one island, behind another, and over to another before heading for their camp.

"I don't think they're behind us now," Ron said panting.

"Nor I. It is extremely doubtful that they could have followed our somewhat devious course."

"What's going on?" Eldon asked again, his voice rising. "Or are you just trying to scare me? Well, I can tell you right now, it won't work!"

"I sure wish Danny and your dad would get back," Ron said fervently. "It wouldn't be so bad if they were here."

Eldon's face went white. "You do mean it, don't you?"

They were gliding silently into the little cove near their camp. Newton looked back over his shoulder to satisfy himself that Hank and Fred had not followed them.

"All clear, Red?"

"Clear for the moment. And with no sign of impending danger."

"I think we'd better pull our canoe up into that thick clump of brush and hide it," Ron observed. "There's no need in advertising that we're here."

"A capital suggestion, Ronald."

"What's this all about?" Eldon asked plaintively, as they carried the canoe up into the brush.

"I wish we could tell you, Eldon," Ron said, "but we've promised not to say anything to anyone until later. Just as soon as we can we'll tell you everything. But right now, we've got to hide our canoe so no one can see it. That's the most important thing right now."

"You aren't feeding me a line, are you?"

"I wish we were," Newton said firmly. "I honestly wish we were."

"Then you're scared too?"

Newton looked at him suspiciously. "Not exactly scared. I do not care for that word. Let us say that I am quite concerned."

"Don't let him kid you, Eldon," Ron said laughing. "He's as scared as I am!"

Even as he spoke Newton stopped suddenly. His mouth dropped open and he swallowed hard.

"Ronald!" he exclaimed. "We're too late!"

"What do you mean?"

For answer Newton pointed. There, almost at his feet, was a boat hidden in the brush!

"Someone has already located our camp," he said. His hands were shaking almost as much as his voice. "They have hidden their boat and are undoubtedly lying in wait for us at this very moment."

Ron looked at the boat.

"You mean that?" he asked laughing. "It's really an old-timer, Red. It's probably all that was left by some trapper or wandering woodsman. It's at least 25 years old."

Newton mopped his brow. "And I have aged at least 25 years. I hope you make the next discovery. I doubt that my nerves will be able to stand much more."

They covered their canoe carefully with leaves and twigs and went back up the slope to camp.

"You know, Red," Ron whispered as they walked, "you'd better find a good hiding place for your camera and the developing equipment. With Hank and Fred in the area we can't be too careful."

"Our thoughts travel along similar lines," Newton answered.

It was Eldon's turn to cook. While he was fixing supper on the little gas stove, Ron and Newton climbed up the big, rock-covered hill and found a place to hide the film and camera on the other side of the slope.

"Now we have it secreted away," Newton said, getting to his feet. "It is safe from prying eyes."

"If we were just safe from prying eyes everything would be shipshape," Ron said.

Newton looked at him reprovingly. "You have the most disgusting habit of calling to mind the most disgusting things, Ronald. There are times when I'm positively ashamed of you." He lowered his voice, "But I do wish that hole in the rocks were a little larger. Large enough for me to creep in, that is."

"And why you?" Ron demanded. "My hide isn't any tougher than yours."

"That is beside the point. Since I am the one who knows how to develop the film. I am the most valuable. I am the one who should be carefully hidden from Hank and Fred."

Then they both laughed.

By the time they returned to the camp Eldon had finished preparing supper. They ate, had their devotions, and went to bed, almost before the sun went down.

"I'm not going to bed yet," Eldon said petulantly, "and it's too cold to sit up without a fire. I'm going to build one."

"Oh, no!" Ron exclaimed quickly. "We can't risk that!"

"But I'd just build a little one."

"That's all we need," Ron told him. "A fire. Then we'd be sure to have company."

Newton nodded in agreement.

"If those guys are going to give us any trouble," Ron continued whispering, "they'll do it tonight. Once they locate us, they're going to move, and move fast."

If the two men had seen the boys and knew where they were camping, they did not molest them. Both Ron and Newton felt relieved when they awakened the following morning.

"See," Eldon said scornfully, "Hank and Fred are just up here fishing. If they are the ones we saw yesterday, they aren't out after us."

"Well," Ron answered, "if I am to be fooled, then that is the way I prefer it. It's a nice way to be fooled."

"Yes," Newton broke in, stepping out of the umbrella tent that served as a dark room, "and I have discovered a very nice way to be fooled too. Instead of being out of film, as we thought we were, I discovered two full magazines."

"What can you take with two little magazines full of film on a project like this?" Eldon demanded, still surly.

"Not much, but if they happen to be of the proper subjects and exposed in the proper manner they could be of some value to our project."

"You don't mean it, Red," Ron said. "No, you couldn't."

"You speak in riddles, Ronald."

"You aren't thinking that we ought to go out after some pictures? Not with Hank and Fred snooping around."

"We do not have to expose ourselves unduly," Newton said. "We can paddle quite swiftly across the half mile of open water to the mainland, and do a bit of exploration in the hopes of finding something worthy of our film."

"O.K.," Ron said. "But it sounds risky to me."

They lit the gasoline stove and cooked breakfast. Ron made sandwiches for lunch while Newton did the dishes. It was still early in the morning when they paddled across the lake and up a small, unnamed creek looking for wildlife.

"If Hank and his pal come over this way looking for us," Ron said, shuddering at the thought, "we won't have a chance of getting away. We'll be dead ducks."

"Danny informed me that he had discovered signs of bear over here," Newton answered. "And we know they want some bear pictures."

"That's one picture I'd as soon not get," Ron told him.

"I think," Eldon announced, "that I'll stay in the canoe."

They had traveled half a mile or more up the narrow creek when Ron spied some bear tracks in the soft mud. "There's a cub around here, fellows," he said, lowering his voice.

"That's the only kind of bear I'd want to meet up with," Eldon muttered under his breath. "A little one."

Newton reached for his camera, while Ron nosed the canoe ashore.

"Are you sure it's safe?" Eldon asked, hesitating uncertainly.

"A bear cub never killed anybody," Newton told him.

"No," Ron put in, "but plenty of mama bears have spread guys all over the landscape because they wanted to play with baby bears."

He saw, almost at a glance, that the tracks were fresh. And they had gone only about two hundred yards when he caught a glimpse of the little cub, ambling aimlessly among the trees.

"Get down, fellows!" he whispered cautiously. "There's the cub! And the chances are that the old mother bear isn't too far away."

"Oh, that will make a striking picture!" Newton exclaimed, fumbling with his camera.

They crept stealthily through the brush. When they were almost within film-shooting range, the cub turned abruptly and began to climb a big tree.

"Look, Ronald!" Newton moaned. "He's up among the branches so we won't be able to see him."

"Maybe he'll come down after a while."

They waited fifteen minutes, but the cub gave no indication of returning to the ground.

"Isn't there something we can do?" Newton asked at last.

Ron glanced carefully about. "I don't see anything of that old bear, do you?"

Newton shook his head.

"Why?"

"That little guy isn't very high. If I thought his mama wasn't around, I'd get him down and give him this apple. Then we could get our pictures."

"Do you suppose you could?" Newton asked hopefully.

Ron darted swiftly forward. It was only a scant

30 feet to the tree the little bear had climbed. He reached it in a dozen strides.

"Now, you little rascal," he said, taking hold of the cub, "come on down here where we can see you."

The cub squealed in protest.

There was a deep-throated roar behind Ron. And a split second later the angered mother bear came charging out of the woods!

"Look out, Ron!" Newton shouted hoarsely. "Run!"

CHAPTER 13

A WILD RIDE!

Ron glanced desperately around. The big bear was a scant ten yards away. Her mouth was open, exposing large yellow fangs, and her little pointed ears were back.

There was no chance to run. No time to dash to another tree and climb it. The bear was almost upon him. Frantically, Ron lunged upward, grasped the lowest limb and hoisted himself upward.

"Hurry, Ron!" Newton shouted. "Hurry!"

But he didn't have to be told that. He scrambled up the tree. And just in time. The bear threw herself at him savagely, slashing at him with her claws. Her great paw just grazed his hip.

Ron's knees bit into the rough bark and he climbed upward before the old bear was able to spring again. The cub, frightened and bewildered by all the noise, pressed close against Ron's leg.

"Go on!" he said sternly, trying to push the cub away with his foot. "I'm not your mother! Go down there where she is! She's the one who wants you!"

Instead, the cub only inched closer to him. The old bear was frantic. Her deep-throated roar reverberated through the forest.

"Get that cub and throw him down to her, Ron!" Newton shouted. "If you don't, you'll have company up there and I don't think you'll like it!"

"I can't do that," Ron answered. "I don't want to hurt the little fellow. He hasn't done anything to me."

"No, but his mama would like to. Throw him down, Ronald!"

The old bear crouched and sprang at the tree, her great paws slapped angrily within inches of Ron's foot. Once or twice, she drove her claws deep into the bark and managed to climb a foot or so off the ground before falling back.

"I'm glad this tree's too small for her to climb!"

"Me too! A couple of times there it looked as though she were going to manage it," shouted Newton. Ron mopped the perspiration from his forehead with the back of his hand. The old bear was getting wilder momentarily. Newton was busy shooting film. Ron could hear the clicking of the shutter – between growls, as it were.

"Why don't you jump down, Ronald," Newton suggested "and make a dash for it?"

"Make a run for it?" Ron was horrified. "Are you in your right mind, Red? I wouldn't get 10 feet."

"No," Newton yelled back, "but we'd sure get some remarkable pictures."

"I've got a better idea. Why don't you guys move around on the other side so you'll be downwind from her? Then Mrs. Bruin will take after you, and junior and I can climb down at our leisure."

"Do you suppose she would take after us if she smelled us?" Eldon wanted to know.

"Not if she didn't like the way you smelled," Ron said.

"You're a big help."

The old bear had almost exhausted herself by lunging at Ron. Now she circled frantically around the tree.

"Go on!" Ron shouted at the cub. "Go down to your mama where you belong! I don't like you anymore!"

"He doesn't mind you, Ronald!" Newton yelled. "Or maybe he thinks you are his mother!"

"If the little rascal doesn't get out of here, I'm going to make like his mother and spank him." Ron turned his attention back to the cub. "Now get out of here and leave me alone."

But the cub only moved closer to him.

Ron should have known better. The first thing Danny and his dad had taught him about bears was that he should never molest a cub. This was all his own fault.

He looked around. If only there were something Red and Eldon could do to attract the mother bear's attention. But, no! That would never work. And besides, it would mean putting them in jeopardy. There had to be another way.

And then he noticed another tree nearby, so close that the branches intertwined.

"I'm going to climb over into this other tree, Red. She'll never leave this one as long as her precious cub is in it."

"Are you sure you can negotiate the transfer, Ronald?" Newton wondered. There was concern in his voice.

"Make it? I've got to!"

Ron began to move carefully around the tree toward the heaviest branch he could find that led out into the other tree. The cub edged after him.

"You're not supposed to go along! Get back there!" He kicked at the little bear gently with his foot, but it continued to follow him. "Shoo! Go back where you belong!"

The big bear moved around the tree.

"How are you managing?" Newton shouted.

"This ornery little guy does think I'm his mother."

"Now get back there where you belong! Get out of here! Shoo!"

The cub hesitated, but only until Ron turned and started to move again. He could almost reach the branch of the other tree. Another foot – another six inches and – suddenly, and without warning, there was a sharp cracking noise.

The limb was breaking off the trunk!

"Help!" Ron cried in desperation. "Help, somebody! Help!"

Ron tried to throw himself forward to catch the branch of the other tree, but his fingers just missed. Down he dropped!

The old bear was standing beneath him, still eying her cub. There was no chance for her to get out of the way. Ron hit her squarely when he dropped, straddling her backwards.

"Help!" he shrieked wildly. "Help!"

His voice was drowned in the yelp of terror from the old bear. With a powerful leap she took off, breaking into a dead run. Ron dug his heels into the startled bear's sides.

"Hang on, Ronald!" Newton shouted. "Hang on! I'm getting some excellent pictures!"

But neither the bear nor Ron were particularly interested in pictures at the moment. She bounced over deadfalls and boulders, wailing like a banshee, with Ron clinging desperately to her back.

"What are we going to do?" Eldon demanded of Newton.

The other boy had already pushed ahead and was climbing to the top of the hill after them. The noise stopped suddenly.

Freight seized Eldon and Newton. "Do you suppose she got him?" Eldon asked.

"She has scarcely had time to eat him," Newton observed, "and if she hurt him, he took it bravely. Without making a sound."

"I knew we should never have come up into this wild country. I knew it."

By this time, they had reached the top of the hill and could look down into the narrow creek on the other side. There, sitting in water up to his armpits, was Ron.

"Are you hurt?" Newton asked.

Slowly, deliberately, Ron stood. The murky swamp water ran in little rivulets off his arms and his clothes. He came out of the creek, his shoes squishing water at every step, and moved toward them.

"Are you alright?" Eldon asked, voice trembling.

"I have something for each of you," Ron managed. "A little souvenir." He handed each of them a small fistful of hair from the back of the old mother bear.

"Why didn't you tell us you were going for a ride, Ronald?" Newton said sternly. "I almost missed getting a picture of that."

"I can tell you one thing," Ron answered, still speaking slowly and without cracking a smile. "If I'd known what it was like I wouldn't have done it. Frankly, riding a bear is for the birds!"

* * *

The following morning the boys were surprised to see Tex circle their camp and touch down on the lake in front of them.

"I've got your film, fellows," he said cheerily. "But where are Danny and Gil?"

"They went back to Angle Inlet for more film," Ron said. "We thought they'd be back last night, but they didn't show up."

The smile left Tex Williams' face.

"I've got the film with me," he said. "I understood Danny wanted me to bring any packages directly up here. I suppose they're sitting back home waiting for it."

"Maybe you can stop by our place and tell them," Ron said. "We sure would like them back here."

"What's the matter, Ron?" Tex asked, laughing. "Are you afraid the bears'll get you?"

"You can say that again."

For the first time since Eldon had been with them, he snickered a little.

"Seriously, Ron," Tex said, "I'm afraid I won't be at Angle Inlet for two or three days. My substitute is taking care of the mail and I've got to go to Kenora and pick up a couple of engineers who're heading for a mining camp. Then I've got to go up into the Red Lake country and get two or three fishermen and take them back to Kenora. It'll take me a couple of days."

When he was gone, Eldon turned to Ron and Newton. "Why didn't you tell Tex about Hank and Fred if you're so scared of them?"

"Don't you see, Eldon?" Ron answered. "We can't tell anybody. Not yet, anyway."

Eldon went back to the camp, and Ron and Newton carried the film to the hideout.

"I wish Tex would get Danny and Gil Pemberton back here right away," Ron said. "I still don't like the idea of being here all by ourselves. Not while Hank and Fred are around."

Newton did not answer him. He was busy examining the package Tex had brought.

"Pause a moment, Ronald," he said. "I am of the opinion that there is some sort of communication from Dr. Desmond in here."

Ron glanced over his shoulder to see a tiny, almost infinitesimal mark in ink beside the address and first-class-mail stamp.

"Dr. Desmond indicated before I left that he would mark any package of film in this manner when he put a note inside."

"Hurry it up, Red!" Ron told him.

Newton tore away the outer wrapper carefully and turned it over.

"What's the matter?" Ron demanded.

His companion's face went white.

"Just about everything," Newton whispered. "Someone broke into the laboratory back in Minneapolis and pilfered a batch of raw film."

Ron moaned his dismay.

"It isn't as bad as all that," Newton hastened to tell him. "They've got raw film so they know some of the secrets, but until they learn how the film is developed, they actually can't do anything."

Ron sighed his relief. "For a minute you had me scared."

"But don't you perceive what this can mean, Ronald?" Newton asked. "Hank and Fred will be more anxious than ever to get us. They are aware of the fact that we are able to develop the film, Eldon told them."

Ron felt all the strength drain out of him. For a moment or two they sat there, staring at one another.

At last Ron spoke.

"We'd better stash away this film and get back before Eldon gets panicky and starts up here after us."

They hid the film and hurried down to the camp.

"I think we ought to move, Red," Ron said as they approached the tents. "We can find a place farther back from the lake – a spot that's more secluded."

"A capital suggestion, Ronald. But a move might make our camp impossible for Danny and Gil to find."

"I–," Ron stopped. "Say, it's awfully quiet here."

"Eldon happens to be alone," Newton told him. "You wouldn't expect him to be conversing with himself, would you?"

"I'm just jumpy, I guess."

A moment later they had reached the tent that served as a dark room.

"There you are!" a rough voice exclaimed. "We almost had to come out after you!"

Newton and Ron whirled to face Hank Green and Fred Havens. The two men were grinning at them evilly.

They had already tied Eldon's hands behind his back and had bound his mouth with a hankie.

"Come on, Newton!" Ron shouted. "Run for it!"

Before Ron covered 10 feet, Fred bounded forward and grabbed him.

"Now don't try any funny stuff," the man ordered angrily, "and nobody will get hurt!"

CHAPTER 14

A WELL-MARKED TRAIL

Hank Green grabbed Newton and jerked him back. "Oh, no, you don't!" He turned to his companion. "This is the one we want, Fred. He's the kid who's been in with old Desmond and has been developing that film."

Newton gulped hard.

"But what're we going to do with the other two?" Fred wanted to know. "We can't be slowed down with all three of them. We've got to make tracks!"

"We can leave them here."

Fred strode over to the knapsack Newton had suspended from a tree and jerked it down. "The developing agents are still here. Come on, Hank, we've got what we need now. Let's go!"

"What do you intend to do with me?" Newton asked, his voice quavering.

"If you do as we tell you, everything'll be all right!" Hank snarled.

"But where are you going to take me?" the boy persisted.

Ron stood motionless while the two men put Newton in the canoe between them.

"Just a minute, Hank," Fred said, shoving his paddle into tire water to hold the heavy canoe close to shore. "These kids have a canoe here. We've got to find it!"

Hank stepped nimbly from the canoe and went charging into the brush.

"Here it is!" he shouted.

He had taken a hand ax with him. Cursing, he threw aside the branches and leaves and went to work. With half a dozen blows of the sharp ax he cut as many ugly holes in the gleaming aluminum craft.

"There!" Hank said, panting. "They won't be able to follow us in that!"

"Better make sure," Fred called. "You know how much is at stake!"

"O.K." This time Hank did not stop until the whole length of the canoe was crisscrossed with holes. "Now, I'd like to see anybody make her float!"

"You didn't have to do that," Ron exclaimed hotly. "You could have taken it with you to some other island. You didn't have to ruin our canoe!"

"Now you know that we mean business. And when that brother of yours and Gil Pemberton get back, you'd better tell them that if they know what's good for them they'll leave us alone!"

"But what are you going to do with Newton?"

"We're not going to hurt him, if that's what you're afraid of."

Eldon, still tied and gagged, struggled desperately to attract Ron's attention. But it was not until the heavy canoe moved out of sight that Ron remembered him.

"I'm sorry, Eldon," he said, kneeling beside the boy and cutting the rope that bound him.

Eldon rubbed his wrists gingerly.

"What about Newton?" he asked. "What's going to happen to him?"

"I wish I knew," Ron exclaimed miserably. "And the worst of it is that we can't do a thing. Not a single thing."

"I didn't believe you guys when you said you were scared of Hank and Fred. But they came charging in here five minutes after you two left and started giving me the third degree about this film. I tried to tell them I didn't know anything about it, but they wouldn't believe me."

"I guess it won't hurt to tell you the whole story now," Ron said. "The worst has already happened. We would have told you before, but Newton had promised Dr. Desmond that he wouldn't tell anyone except Danny and me."

As he spoke, the color drained from Eldon's thin cheeks.

"So that's the reason you were so shook when I spilled the beans about your film back at Angle Inlet."

Ron nodded.

"Then I'm the one who's to blame! I caused this whole rotten mess!"

"Right now, the important thing is to figure out something to help Newton get away from those men. They said they weren't going to hurt him, but I don't trust them."

"But what can we do?"

Silently Ron began to pray.

Ron scarcely realized that he had bowed his head and closed his eyes until Eldon broke in roughly.

"What are you doing?" he demanded. "Praying again?" Ron finished before he looked up.

"It's the most important thing we can do right now."

Eldon eyed him queerly. "Does it really help? To pray, I mean?"

"That all depends," Ron answered.

"On what?" interest and suspicion in his voice.

"Whether you have taken the Lord Jesus as your Savior," Ron went on. "The Bible is full of promises for the Christian, but there is only one prayer an unbeliever can offer and be sure that God will answer it."

Doubt clouded Eldon's eyes. "What's that?"

"'God be merciful to me, a sinner.' No one has ever prayed that prayer without an answer. God always forgives every unbeliever who comes to Him in repentance."

"Every one?" Eldon echoed. "Every *single* one?"

"That's right. 'Him that cometh unto me, I will in no wise cast out,' He tells us. 'The wages of sin is death, but the gift of God is eternal life through Jesus Christ our Lord.' "

Eldon sighed deeply.

"Wouldn't you like to get right with God, Eldon?" Ron insisted gently.

The boy ran his fingers nervously through his hair.

"Some time, maybe," he said. "But not now. I've got plenty of time."

" 'Behold now is the accepted time . . . Now is the day of salvation.' That's what the Bible tells us. You don't know whether there's plenty of time or not."

Eldon hesitated for a long minute.

"I guess you're right, Ron," he said at last, stumbling over the words.

Together the two boys squatted on the grass and Ron explained the way of salvation, step by step. Then they knelt, and Eldon prayed under Ron's direction.

* * *

It was sometime later that the boys got to their feet and turned their attention once more to Newton. Strange, but concern for him had been shoved aside momentarily.

"I want you to know how sorry I am for the way I treated you and Newton," Eldon said. "I guess I disliked you because you seemed so happy and contented.

And I was neither. But I envied you too. Those verses you read and quoted to me would ring in my heart for hours, and there were some nights I could scarcely get to sleep."

"I know," Ron answered. "It's been a long time since I accepted the Lord, but I remember I was the same way."

He walked slowly down to the shore of the lake and looked out across the placid water. It was midafternoon, but the wind had gone down and the lake looked like a mirror around the island.

"If only Hank and Fred hadn't ruined our canoe."

Eldon straightened suddenly. "Ron," he said, tensely, "what about that old boat? Do you suppose we could patch it?"

"Now you're in gear, Eldon!" Ron exclaimed.

Together they ran into the brush where they had found the old boat earlier in the day.

"Help me get it turned over."

They struggled to lift the boat on its side. It was made out of planking, and the boards were dry and warped.

"I think we can do it, Eldon! I think we can do it!"

They turned the boat on its gunwales and Ron began to go over the bottom carefully.

"We'll need some pitch and moss, Eldon," he said without looking up. "Maybe you can get those things while I drive in some of these nails."

The boys worked frantically on the little boat, forcing moss and pine pitch into the cracks.

"There," Ron said at last, wiping the perspiration from his forehead, "I think we're ready to go!"

"But where? That's what I want to know."

"If I know Newton Jonathan Edward Bostwick III," Ron told him, "he'll leave some sort of a trail for us to follow."

They put the old boat into the water and Ron and Eldon began to paddle. It was cumbersome, unwieldy, and leaked freely, but they bailed it out with an empty pork-and-beans can and were able to paddle along the rushes toward the end of the island.

"See," Ron said after a few minutes, "Newton has been breaking reeds to show us that they came this way."

"And there's a piece of a gum wrapper," Eldon pointed out.

"And there's something else on the water 40 or 50 yards out," Ron added excitedly. "See, what did I tell you!"

"It's a good thing that guy liked to eat," Eldon muttered. "Gum wrappers and paper off candy! He must have had his pockets full."

"I knew he'd leave a trail. Those guys'll never be able to get ahead of him."

It was almost dark by the time the boys had followed Newton's trail across the lake to the portage the men had taken.

"It'll be easier to follow them now," Ron said. "At least as long as they stay on land."

Ron moved four or five steps up from the lake and was standing directly in the path, sniffing the air.

"Smell anything?"

"Should I?"

"Don't you smell pine smoke?"

Eldon sniffed.

Ron grinned. "A lot of help you are. I know that someone has built a fire up ahead. I'm sure of it."

"Maybe it's somebody else," Eldon suggested, almost hopefully. "Those fellows won't start a fire out here when they've kidnapped Newton. They won't want to attract attention."

"Don't forget they think we're back on the island. And they know that Danny and your dad wouldn't be flying around at night. No, they'll be fixing a good warm meal tonight because they'll think they won't have one tomorrow night. That's when they'll really be on the dodge."

The two boys crept forward stealthily. Every dozen paces or so, Newton had managed to leave a mark. Here he had broken a twig with his foot; there he had scratched a birch tree with the blunt edge of his knife.

"That smoke's smelling stronger all the time, Eldon," Ron said.

His companion nodded. "Even I can smell it now."

They hadn't gone more than a hundred yards farther when Eldon stopped and sucked in his breath sharply.

There on the trail ahead of them was a campfire. "Look, Ron!"

Ron crept forward and Eldon followed. There was Newton sitting cross-legged before the little fire. Hank was busy with the skillet over the fire, and Fred was suspending their knapsacks and food from the branches of a tree.

"What are we going to do now, Ron?" Eldon whispered.

CHAPTER 15

RESCUE ATTEMPT

For a long minute Ron and Eldon crouched there, staring at Newton and the men who had captured him.

"They haven't tied Newton up," Ron whispered. "If he had half a chance and knew we were out here he could get away."

"If we could just attract his attention."

Ron thought for a moment. "I've got it," he whispered, more to himself than his companion. "Old Red knows that I'm pretty good with a slingshot. If I can hit him on the hand with something he'll know that we're out here. Then when Fred and Hank are asleep, he can make a run for it."

"And where are you going to get the slingshot?"

Ron took his Bible from the pocket of his jacket and slipped the inner-tube band off the buckskin case.

"Cut me a forked stick," he ordered, fishing his scout knife from his pocket.

In a few minutes he had a very acceptable slingshot.

"And now for some ammunition." He cut a few pointed bits of wood from a nearby branch. "Now," he continued, "we'll see whether Red catches on or not."

They were still 50 feet or so from the little camp site, and had been talking in signs and whispers.

Ron took a small handful of wood pellets, motioned for Eldon to follow him, and began to crawl with all the stealth that Danny had taught him. The clearing was small and the cover so thick that there was a small chance of hitting Newton, unless they managed to get very close.

It was dark now. Pitch dark. And the little campfire was so small that it only gave a tiny flicker of light.

"I tell you we shouldn't have left those other two kids back on the island," Hank said grumbling. "What if that older Orlis and Gil Pemberton come back? They've got the plane and the kids are there to tell them what happened to Bostwick. We'll have the Mounties on our trail in no time."

"The first thing we're going to do is make this kid tell us how to develop that film," Fred answered. "Then we'll have what we came after, and we can clear out of here before they have time to call in the Mounties or anyone else."

"When are you going to make him develop film for us?" Hank insisted. "That's what I want to know. Every hour we're out here is just that much too long."

"We'll get it. Don't worry about that. There's no

sense in going to work on him until we get over to where we hid the plane." He glanced over at Newton ominously. "When I start in on him, he'll be glad enough to show us how to develop that film. And fast."

"What makes you so sure that a smart guy like Dr. Desmond would trust a secret like this to a kid?"

"I will have you to understand, gentlemen," Newton told them, "that I am no 'kid' in the accepted meaning of the term. In fact, I believe I am quite safe in saying that I am not a 'kid' in any meaning of the term. I am a close friend and associate of Dr. Desmond, helping him with certain formulae used in the development of his revolutionary color film. And the last time I looked in the mirror I noticed a distinct, if scattered, growth of whiskers on my upper lip. I should not be surprised if I would be shaving regularly in another year or so."

"Oh, shut up!" Hank snorted. "When we want anything from you we'll ask for it."

Ron drew back his slingshot and let fly. The pellet missed Newton by a foot.

"I thought you said you were a good shot with that thing," Eldon whispered.

"I've got to get zeroed in," Ron whispered back. "You just wait until I get the range."

He placed another pellet in the sling and drew back again, as far as he dared. This time he nailed Newton on the back of his neck, just above the collar on his jacket.

"Ouch!" the boy cried suddenly.

"Now what's the matter with you?" Hank wanted to know.

"Something stung me!" He was rubbing the back of his neck.

"You're imagining things," Fred broke in. "There isn't anything out here that would–"

Ron took careful aim and let fly again.

"Ouch!"

Both men were staring at Newton.

"I tell you something's biting me!" he cried. "It got me on the ear that time!"

"I don't know what you're trying to pull," Fred snarled, "but I can tell you this much, it isn't going to do you any – Ouch!"

"Now what's eating you?" Hank growled.

"I tell you, I felt it too!"

"What did I tell you?" Newton asked. "Something bit me very severely on the neck and on the ear."

"It must be them 'no-see-ums,' the Indians were telling us about."

"I can tell you one thing," Newton observed, "they most assuredly are not 'no-feel-ums.' "

Eldon turned to Ron and snickered.

"I don't know what's the matter with that guy," Ron said. "You'd think he'd wise up after a while."

"Maybe you ought to use a rock," Eldon whispered.

"If this slingshot would throw one big enough, I would."

"Here," Eldon whispered, "let me try."

Ron handed the slingshot to his companion.

There was another trick Newton had told about several times. One that he had used on a scout trip to give his pals a bad time. He'd be sure to recognize it.

Eldon scored a hit on Hank. The big fellow let out a bellow of rage.

"You are in good voice, sir," Newton said seriously. "Extremely good voice. Did anyone ever tell you that you have all the resonance of a bull moose?"

Hank glared at him. "I think you've got something to do with this, kid," he said ominously. "And if you have it'll be too bad for you."

"You want to remember," Newton reminded him, "that this nefarious creature, whatever it is, vented its anger on me first."

Ron had crept back from the campsite while this was going on, and cut a long, willowy branch with his scout knife, trimming off the twigs and leaves. Then he cut several thin strips of leather from the flap of the case in which he carried his Bible, and with them he tied the knife securely to the end of the stick.

"What are you going to do with that thing?" Eldon whispered as he came back.

"You wait and see."

When Ron had everything ready, he began to creep closer to the tree. Hank, Fred, and Newton had started to eat supper. They were sitting around the fire.

Ron had made his way behind the tree from which

they had suspended their grub and several knapsacks. Cautiously Ron reached out with the stick and began to saw on the rope with the knife.

"They'll see you, Ron," Eldon warned.

But Ron acted as though he hadn't even heard him. A moment or two later, the rope began to stretch as the last strand was cut. The pack dropped with a thud. Both men jumped to their feet.

"What was that?" Hank demanded.

"You just didn't tie up that knapsack good enough," Fred told him. "I don't know why you couldn't do a little thing like that and do it right."

"Maybe you can fix them yourself the next time. Then they'll be put up to suit you."

"Right now, I'm going to finish eating."

They left the sack where it had fallen.

Ron looked at Newton, but the boy acted as though he hadn't even seen him. He kept right on eating.

Ron moved forward half a step and began to saw the rope that held the second pack. In a couple of minutes, it too fell to the ground.

"There goes another one! You'd better go over and take that third one down, or it'll fall too."

"If you want it down, suppose you go over and take it down yourself. Nobody's holding you."

The two men began to argue. But still Newton did not look up.

"What's the matter with that guy anyway?" Ron demanded. "He still doesn't know we're around."

"We're going to fool around here and get caught," Eldon whispered.

Ron reached out for the rope that suspended the third sack. It was so far out on the limb that he couldn't quite reach it. He climbed up on the stump of a deadfall and reached out with his knife and stick.

It was slow, tedious work.

At last Newton looked up and his eyes widened.

"Oh, no!" he exclaimed. "That pack's got my binoculars in it!"

Ron was so startled that he lost his balance and went sprawling forward to the ground.

"Those kids!" Hank shouted.

CHAPTER 16

"HELP! HELP!"

Ron scrambled to his feet and started to dash into the woods, but he was not in time. Hank leaped towards him, cursing. He grabbed him by the collar of his shirt and almost jerked him down.

"Oh, no, you don't! Not this time!"

He turned to face Newton. "And don't you try any funny stuff. I can handle both of you."

Fred had raced past them and had disappeared among the trees.

"What was the big idea, Red?" Ron demanded. "Why did you shout like that?"

"I'm quite sorry, Ronald," Newton explained. "I completely forgot myself when I saw you cutting the rope on my knapsack. A drop like that could have demolished my binoculars and they're the only ones I own."

"That neck of yours is the only one you own too.

That yell of yours sure put it in hock. And mine too, when you get right down to it."

"Shut up, you guys!" Hank snarled.

By this time, Fred came striding back to the campsite, shoving Eldon ahead of him.

"Try to get away from me again and you'll be mighty sorry!" he warned. "Now get over there with your buddies and don't give us any trouble."

Hank's ugly face darkened. "How did you guys get away from that island?" he demanded harshly.

"What difference does that make now?" Fred broke in. "We've got to learn how to develop that film and get out of here. But fast!"

Hank was still facing Ron and Eldon. "I told you fellows that you wouldn't get hurt if you didn't try to follow us. Now I'm going to teach you a lesson you won't forget in a hurry."

"Don't do anything to them," Newton said. "I'm the person you want. They aren't able to help you develop that film. They know nothing whatever about it."

"If you don't want to see them hurt, you'd better get busy and develop that film pronto."

"I thought we were going to wait until we get to the plane," Fred countered.

"I changed my mind." Hank took a step or two backward, as though to take down Newton's knapsack. "I didn't say anything to you about it because I knew you'd howl, but I've been figuring on flying this kid to Winnipeg, making him develop the film in my dark room, and turning him loose. But we can't take *three* kids that far."

"Now you're talking sense. Let's get this info and get out of here."

"I would like very much to accommodate you," Newton said, "but I am sorry to have to inform you that I cannot complete the process here. It is very complicated, and I lack certain ingredients."

"Don't lie to me!" Hank stormed over to the tree, untied the knapsack and tossed it to Newton.

"Don't do that!" Newton shouted in dismay. "My binoculars!"

"Your binoculars!" Ron snorted. "I hope they do get busted."

"Now, Ronald," Newton cautioned. "Temper. Temper."

Ron grinned in spite of the mess they were in.

"I know you've got the stuff in here to develop that film," Hank exclaimed. "Now get in my tent and get busy. And remember, I'll be standing right behind you. I'm a commercial photographer so you won't be able to fool me. You'd better do it right!"

"As I have been trying to tell you, I do not have either the facilities or the material to develop the film."

The tall man opened the knapsack almost angrily. "There's a bottle marked solution 1. This one is 2, this 3, this 4, and so on. Are those bottles for developing film, or aren't they?"

"At one time they have been," Newton admitted.

"All right. Get busy and be quick about it."

"I'm going to tie up these other two kids while you and Bostwick are fiddling with that film," Fred said. "I'm not having them pull anything on me."

Fred bound Ron's and Eldon's hands securely, while Newton and Hank were busy in the tent.

"Why didn't Newton hide all the developing solutions?" Eldon whispered.

Ron shook his head, and motioned for the boy to keep quiet.

"O heavenly Father," he began to pray, "we're in a terrible mess. Help us to get out of it safely, and help us, in some way, to protect Dr. Desmond's secret processes so Hank and Fred cannot steal his new color film…."

When he looked up, he saw that Eldon was watching him.

"I've been praying too," the other boy said.

Inside the tent Newton got out his solutions.

"This is only a waste of time, I am sorry to inform you. Nothing is going to come of it."

"Something had better come of it!" Hank retorted, cursing.

"Do you have a piece of exposed film? I neglected to bring any along."

"Yes, I have some exposed film, but be careful with it. I've got one other piece."

"Then I would suggest that you keep it safe," Newton said again. "This will only ruin it."

"Shut up and get to work."

Newton unrolled the film carefully in the pitch dark of the little tent.

"Should I explain what I am doing as I go along?"

"I want any information I'll need to duplicate the process."

Newton went through the process, step by step. "And now," he said, "we are ready to put the film to the test. Of course, it won't do any good, but I suppose you'll never be satisfied until you've seen for yourself."

Hank almost jerked the film from his hands and switched on a powerful flashlight.

"Bostwick!" he cried, cursing. "I ought to work you over proper! You've lied to me! You didn't develop this the way you normally do!"

"What's the matter?" Fred demanded, joining them.

"This impudent kid! I ought to–"

"I told you we couldn't develop the film here, that we lacked certain ingredients, but you insisted on it. Here." Newton thrust one of the solution bottles into the man's hand. "Taste it."

Something about his voice compelled Hank to stick his finger into the bottle. "Why it feels like–" Gingerly he tasted it with the tip of his tongue. "It's *water!*"

"Water?" Fred echoed in dismay.

"Water." Hank threw the bottle to the ground. "We've been taken in!" he growled. "By a fool kid!"

"It was rather clever of me too, was it not?" Newton asked impudently. "When I perceived that there was a chance that you might pay us a visit, we hid the proper solutions and our supply of film. And I filled some empty solution bottles with water. That is why I endeavored to keep you from wasting your film."

For a full minute neither of the men spoke.

"What are we going to do?" Fred asked irritably. "Things are really in a mess now."

"There's only one thing we can do. Go back to that island and get the solutions right away. Before Orlis and Pemberton get back there."

"You mean right now?" his companion demanded. "Tonight?"

"Tonight!"

"But I'm tired. All we've been doing since we came up here has been lug canoes, paddle, and walk. I'm tired, Hank. I don't think I can go another step."

"Shut up! You want to get that formula, don't you?" There was a short silence.

"We'll have to tie up those kids until we get back. They've caused us enough trouble already."

"Tie them up and take a chance on their getting away and causing us more trouble?" Hank asked. "Nothing doing. We're going to take them right along with us. Then we'll know what they're doing."

Fred got out a short piece of rope and tied Newton's hands behind him. Then he tied all three boys together, single file, and fastened the loose end of the rope to his own waist.

"Now, you guys can't cause us any trouble on this portage."

"Before we start, you're going to have to give me that formula, Bostwick," Hank said sternly. "And you'd better give it to me straight if you know what's good for you."

"And if I don't?"

"You don't want anything to happen to your pals, do you?"

Reluctantly, Newton told Hank, step by step, how to develop the film, and he wrote it down with a stub of a pencil. When he finished Hank looked up, his dark eyes boring into Newton's.

"This is the way you develop the film?" he asked.

Newton nodded.

"You've told me the truth?"

"I have told you the truth," Newton answered. "But there are certain solutions with which I am unfamiliar. I will have to get them back at our camp. I should say that I am unfamiliar with their formulae, except–" He stopped quickly.

"Except what?"

"Except that Dr. Desmond told me to guard them very carefully, that they could be duplicated by any chemist who managed to get them in his possession." Newton spoke reluctantly.

Hank smiled broadly. "Now it sounds as though we're getting somewhere. It's a good thing that you are a Christian and wouldn't lie to me. That helped, Bostwick. That really helped."

Newton gritted his teeth. "I didn't lie to you," he said. "The film isn't worth that, valuable as it is."

"Well, come on," Fred broke in, "let's get going! We've got some hard miles to cover."

"Too bad you fellows have to carry the canoe all that way," Ron said. "This is going to be the easiest portage I've ever made."

"It isn't so far," Fred retorted.

Hank went over to the canoe. "Come on, Fred! Take hold of your end and let's get on the move."

"But I've got these kids tied to my waist," the other protested.

"Get your end. I'm not going to carry this heavy thing by myself."

"I told you we ought to buy a new aluminum canoe," Fred said grumbling, "but, no, you had to use this old scow. It's like hauling a rowboat around."

Nevertheless, he picked up the back of the canoe and they started through the forest in the darkness.

Ron, who was tied next to Fred, slowed down until the rope was taut.

"Hey, you guys!" Fred complained. "Don't pull back like that. This canoe is heavy enough without having to drag you along too."

Newton, who was behind Ron, poked him in the back. "Give him a rough time, Ronald," he whispered. "It's our only chance."

"What did you say?" Fred asked suspiciously.

"Come on!" Hank ordered. "We've got to make

time if we want to pick up those solutions and get out of there before Orlis and Pemberton fly in."

"These kids are plotting against me, Hank. And I don't like it."

"Those kids can't hurt you any."

"That's what you think."

"You make me tired."

They started on again. Ron and his companions lagged just enough to keep the rope between Fred and him taut. At times he would jerk back, and Fred would stagger along for a few paces trying to keep his balance.

"I don't know what's the matter with you," Hank exclaimed. "You can't even carry your end of the canoe. We never will get back to the lake if you don't do any better than this."

"How can I make time?" his companion wanted to know. "You keep pulling the canoe forward and those ornery kids keep pulling back on me until I can hardly stand up."

"I thought I told you guys to behave yourselves."

"Yes, sir," the boys chorused.

"I mean it."

"Yes, sir."

They started forward once more. Ron walked fast enough to keep the rope slack.

"Now that's more like it," Fred said. "Act like this and we'll all be a lot better off. That's–uh!" he exclaimed as the wind went out of him.

Ron had stopped suddenly.

"Come on, Fred!" Hank said irritably, pulling the canoe forward. "We've got to get to the lake."

Fred staggered and stumbled around, trying to hang onto the canoe and keep his balance.

"Now what?" Hank asked him.

"It's not my fault, I tell you! It's those blasted kids! I just can't do it, Hank. I can't take care of them and help carry the canoe too."

"But you've got to help with the canoe. And we can't untie these kids or they'll give us more trouble."

"This is the easiest portage I've ever made," Ron said.

"Usually we have to help carry stuff, but this time we get a free ride."

"Silence, Ronald," Newton broke in. "We don't want to give them any ideas."

The two men looked at one another.

"Why not?"

"They can't give us any trouble if they're under that canoe," Hank said. "Besides, we'll both be right behind them."

Hurriedly the men untied the hands of the boys and loosened the rope from Fred.

"We can leave them tied together," he suggested. "They won't be able to get far that way."

"What if we refuse to carry the canoe?" Ron asked.

"You'll carry it, all right! Now, get it up and let's move! We've already wasted a lot of time."

The boys turned the canoe over and lifted it, bottom side up, to their shoulders.

"Now stay on the trail, Orlis," Hank ordered. "And remember that we're right behind you."

"This is a gyp," Ron said loudly. "I've got a plan, fellows," he then whispered. "Do as I do when I holler."

"But how'll we know what you're going to–," Eldon started to ask him.

"You guys, up there! Can the talk!"

Another 300 yards and they reached the lake shore.

"I wonder if our boat is still here?" Ron asked aloud.

"Your boat?" Hank exclaimed. "Why didn't we think of that? Here we've carried our canoe all this way for nothing."

"You wouldn't like our boat. It leaks too much. Besides, there isn't room enough for all of us in it."

Eldon and Newton started to put the canoe down, but Ron still gripped it firmly.

"What are we going to do with young Orlis and Pemberton?" Fred demanded. "We can't all ride back to the island."

"We can tie them up and leave them here as soon as I shove this boat out into deep water so it'll drift away. Then we'll know they won't be tagging along."

By this time both men had come around in front of the boys. As Hank stopped and shoved the old wooden scow out into deep water, Ron signaled to his pals.

"Now!"

At that instant Newton and Eldon saw what he planned. They ran forward, hit Hank with the prow of the canoe they were carrying and toppled him into the icy water.

"Help!" he shrieked. "Help!"

Fred saw them coming and tried to duck out of the way, but he was too slow. Eldon swung his end of the canoe around, caught Fred on the shoulder with it and pushed him into the lake too.

The men were shouting, cursing, and splashing.

"Hurry up!" Ron yelled as they dropped the canoe into the water and jumped in. "We've got to get out of here."

He snatched one of the paddles from its holder alongside the canoe and thrust it deeply into the water. Newton did the same. The canoe glided smoothly away.

"Don't take our canoe!" Hank shouted, pulling himself up to the bank. "You can't leave us out here like this!"

"We'll be back just as soon as we can get hold of Danny and Gil," Ron called back to them.

"But we didn't mean those things we said about the film," Fred pleaded. "We were just joking. That was all. We wouldn't think of stealing your film."

"We're just joking too," Eldon put in.

"If you don't come back for us, it'll be too bad for you," Hank threatened. "You just wait and see!"

"I know you fellows are enjoying yourselves," Newton said to Ron and Eldon, "and I dislike to spoil the fun. But it seems expedient to me that we move close enough to shore to get the boat and take it with us – at least out into the middle of the lake. And then I think we ought to be heading back toward camp. Does that sound worthy of your consideration?"

"Indubitably," Ron said grinning. "Indubitably!"

CHAPTER 17

"A CHANCE TO WIN!"

The boys paddled over to the water-logged old boat, some 15 or 20 feet offshore.

"Take hold of her, Eldon," Ron said, "and we'll drag her out into the lake a ways."

"That is an excellent suggestion, Ronald," Newton said, "but–"

He stopped in mid-sentence as Hank whipped off his shoes and dived into the water.

"Let's get out of here!"

They paddled as hard as they could, but the weight of the old boat held them back. They managed to drag it another 30 or 40 feet, when Eldon saw that Hank was almost upon them.

"I'm letting go, fellas!" he shouted.

The swimmer was a scant 10 feet from them when he let go of the boat and the canoe shot ahead.

Fred Havens cursed loudly.

"That was close!" Eldon gasped. "I looked around and there he was, almost ready to grab hold of us."

"Just keep paddling, Red," Ron said, panting heavily, "and we've got it made."

By this time darkness had swallowed the shoreline, and all was silent about them.

"I think we're safe now," Newton said several minutes later.

"We can thank God for that."

"You can say that again," Eldon added fervently.

The silence was deafening.

"Are my ears deceiving me?" Newton asked. "Or am I correct in saying that I just heard you speak, Eldon?"

The boy laughed nervously. "It was me, all right."

Newton quit paddling and Ron did the same.

"I–I don't know quite how to say it," Eldon began, "but I–I–" he swallowed hard. "I'm a Christian now," he blurted.

"That is good news."

"I guess I wanted to take the Lord as my Savior the first time that you guys talked with me about Him," Eldon went on. "I know I felt guilty enough. So guilty that I couldn't even sleep for a couple of nights. But I've confessed my sin and taken Jesus as my Savior."

"It's wonderful, isn't it?"

"I don't feel so much different. Should I?"

"Dad always says that feeling doesn't mean too much," Ron told him. "The feeling will come later. Right now the most important thing is that you've met God's conditions for salvation and have given your heart to the Lord Jesus."

"I've done that, all right," Eldon said with confidence. "And I'm certainly glad it's settled. If that means anything."

They talked on for a few minutes and then began to paddle once more. It was almost dawn when they finally pulled into their camp.

"You know something," Ron said, getting wearily out of the canoe and helping to pull it up on shore. "I'm tired!"

"That is one observation with which I am in complete and hearty agreement."

They dragged themselves up to their camp and dropped into their sleeping bags.

"I know this isn't a pleasant thought," Eldon said, "but what if Hank and Fred come after us in that old boat?"

"Let them come," Ron mumbled sleepily. "I don't think I could even lift a finger to stop them."

"I considered that same possibility," Newton said. "At the rate that craft must have been leaking with you and Ronald in it, I sincerely doubt whether Hank and Fred would risk coming over here in it."

"That moss and pine pitch wouldn't last too long," Ron said. "A lot of it was going out before we got ashore. We worked so fast I'm afraid we didn't do a good job."

"Fortunately."

"And besides, Hank and Fred wouldn't risk

coming over here in daylight again. They know now that Danny and Eldon's dad will be back any time."

"There are times when every man must take a calculated risk," Newton said just before going to sleep. "And insofar as I am concerned, this is one of those times."

The next thing they knew, it was broad daylight and someone was shaking them violently.

"A fine thing!" Danny exclaimed. "Coming back here and finding you guys asleep at noon."

"You don't know the half of it," his brother told him.

When he and Gill heard the story of what had happened the night before, Danny got to his feet quickly. "I think this is something for the Mounties, Gil," he said.

"Do you think we dare leave the boys here with fellows like that around."

Danny laughed a little.

"From the sound of things, they have proved themselves able to take very good care of themselves."

"Only don't stay two or three days this time, Danny," Ron cautioned.

"Do you think those fellows could get very far away, Ron?" Danny asked.

"Not unless they fly. I know they couldn't paddle that leaky old scow any place. And there's so much muskeg over in that area that the portage is about the only high ground around."

Danny and Gil Pemberton took off again, but in an hour they were back.

"The Mounties will be along right away," Danny

said. "They'll take care of those fellows. We won't have to worry about that."

While Ron and Newton were talking with Danny, Eldon called his dad off to one side.

"What's on your mind, son?" Gil asked when they were alone together.

"I know I've given you a rough time the last couple of years, Dad," he began, fumbling for words, "and I–I want to tell you that I'm sorry."

Gil Pemberton stared at him in amazement.

"What did you say?" he asked incredulously.

"I know I'll probably make mistakes and say a lot of things I shouldn't, and do a lot of things I shouldn't," Eldon went on, "but Ron says that I can call on the Lord Jesus for help to do as I ought to, and–"

"What is it you're trying to tell me, Eldon?"

The boy hesitated, gathering courage. "I'm a Christian now, Dad," he said, his voice choked. "And with God's help, I'm going to be the kind of son you've always wanted me to be."

Gil Pemberton was silent. His eyes moistened and he swallowed hard.

"I never thought I'd be glad to hear you say that, son," he said when he could trust his voice again. "But I am. I am."

"What about you, Dad?" Eldon asked softly.

Mr. Pemberton turned quickly away.

* * *

The rest of the picture-taking went smoothly and by the end of the following week they had shot the last scene and packed up to go back to Angle Inlet.

"I shall take the film down to Dr. Desmond," Newton said. "He will make a print for you immediately and have it back in time to meet your deadline with the tourist bureau."

"That sounds great," Danny answered, "if somebody doesn't follow you and take it away from you."

Newton looked at him reprovingly. "Daniel," he said with mock sternness, "you think of the most unpleasant things."

* * *

Danny got the film from Dr. Desmond within a week. He and Gil sent it on to Toronto.

"We'd just as well stick around for a while and do some fishing. Besides, I want Eldon to spend as much time as possible with Ron. He's good for him."

"It isn't Ron who's making the change in Eldon," Danny said, "It's the Lord Jesus."

Gil shook his head.

"It won't last," he said doubtfully. "Nobody could change that much, that fast."

"The apostle Paul was a murderer," Danny answered quietly, "a killer of Christians. After he met the Lord on the Damascus road, he became a fearless follower of Christ."

Gil walked out to the end of the dock arid back again. "If I could believe," he said hoarsely, "that becoming a Christian could make that much difference in Eldon, you'd have yourself another convert."

Two weeks passed, and then Ron got a letter from Newton.

"It will interest you to know, I am sure, that Dr. Desmond made a presentation of his film to the film company executives. On the basis of one showing, they are making him a tentative offer of a royalty contract that will make the contest look small by comparison. Of course, the contract is contingent upon the film proving out under their exhaustive tests. But we know from experience that it will. He also has a chance to win the award. A very good chance...."

"He made it, Danny!" Ron shouted. "He made it!"

Eldon and Gil Pemberton came running.

"Well now, that is something," Gil said smiling broadly. "We got our picture and Dr. Desmond was able to market his film. The trip has worked out very well all the way around."

"I'll say it has," Eldon said.

His dad looked at him quizzically. "I don't think I follow you, son."

"I'm the greatest gainer of all, Dad," the boy explained. "For I took the Lord Jesus as my Savior. I'm a Christian now."

Gil Pemberton's eyes filled quickly, and he turned away. But not before Danny saw.

He motioned to the others to stay behind. And he walked arm and arm with Gil into the Pemberton cabin.

THE DANNY ORLIS SERIES

The Danny Orlis series, by Bernard Palmer, delivers a blend of adventure, mystery, and suspense through various settings—from the Canadian wilderness to Guatemalan jungles. Danny Orlis, an adept outdoorsman, skilled athlete, and committed Christian, employs his quick thinking, calm bravery, and biblical solutions to confront everyday problems and hair-raising dangers. Early stories focus on Danny navigating school life, sports, and outdoor challenges, while in later books, Danny and his wife Kay provide wisdom and guidance to youngsters facing lifelike situations and challenges. Having sold over two million copies, this series has made Palmer a renowned author in Christian youth literature. Palmer is also the author of the Felicia Cartright series and various other series for Christian youth.

AVAILABLE FROM WWW.ANEKOPRESS.COM